TEN CLASSIC INDIAN STORIES

Retold by

Sunita Pant Bansal

Published by—
UNICORN BOOKS PVT. LTD.
F-2/16, Ansari Road, Daryaganj, New Delhi-110002
☎ 011-23262683, 45644782, 23250704
e-mail: info@unicornbooks.in
website: www.unicornbooks.in

ISBN: 978-81-7806-581-6

Printed at : Param Offsetters, Okhla, New Delhi-110020

CONTENTS

PREFACE

Classic Indian Stories, as the name suggests, are timeless classics. A classic story is one that evokes strong emotions and keeps its reader thinking. It has layers of meaning, giving it the ability to generate a continuous discussion.

India has always been, and still is, a country of storytellers. We have a rich repertoire of vernacular classics. We also have a steadily growing percentage of young readers. We, at UNICORN, wanted to introduce the timeless Indian classics to those readers.

This book is a carefully curated collection of stories from Bengali, Odiya, Assamese, Gujarati, Sindhi, Urdu, and Hindi writers, retold in English. The study of these stories would encourage the readers to become familiar with some of the most revered Indian authors, like Bankim Chandra Chatterjee, Rabindranath Tagore, Premchand and so on.

Care has been taken to create a multi-dimensional canvas of stories.

Some stories are fun like the mythological *Suvarna Golak* of Bankim Chandra Chatterjee or husband-wife tiff over *Shaljam* of Saadat Hasan Manto or even the hilariously absurd luck of *The Lucky Brahmin* of Dakshinaranjan Mitra Majumder. But, under the garb of fun is hidden a life lesson in each, for the reader to discover.

Some stories explore the depth of filial relationships like *Kabuliwala* of Rabindranath Tagore, *Daak Munshi* of Fakir Mohan Senapati, and *ThePost Office* of Gaurishankar Govardhanram Joshi 'Dhumketu'. These stories too, go beyond the parent-child relationship, reflecting the social fabric of those times, the class-caste differences, and the subtle impact of westernisation.

Friendship is yet another important relationship of trust and enduring affection between two people. *Sakhi* of Suryakant Tripathi 'Nirala' shows to what extent a bond of friendship can go, while *Addo Abdul Rahman* of Amarlal Hingorani is a friend of the deserving. The definitions of 'extent' and 'deserving' are for the readers to find out.

Bhadaari of Lakshminath Bezbaruah and *Kafan* of Premchand are stories of the poor, the marginalised, seemingly sad, but carrying deep, positive life lessons within.

These ten classic stories will enrich the mind and seed the heart of the reader with compassion.

We have grown up reading and studying western classics in schools; it is high time we look towards our own treasure trove of Indian classics. This book is a step in that direction.

Sunita Pant Bansal

Bankim Chandra Chatterjee *(Chattopadhyay) (1838-1894) was a Bengali poet, novelist, essayist, and journalist. He laid the foundation for the spiritual revival of Bengal, his writings awakening a spirit of self-confidence in the people and pride in their religion and history. Chatterjee had a deep knowledge of Sanskrit literature and incorporated its elements including mythology in his works. He believed in women empowerment and portrayed strong female characters in his writings. He also introduced the concept of historical novel in Bengali literature. Chatterjee's novel* Anand Math *became the source of inspiration for the Indian independence movement. The song* Vande Mataram *from this novel became a rallying cry for freedom fighters, making it the National Song of India. Chatterjee is known as* SahityaSamrat *or Emperor of Literature in Bengal.*

Subarna Golak *is a humorous short story based on the conversation between Shiva and Parvati.*

SUBARNA GOLAK

(THE GOLDEN SPHERE)

A Bengali story

Bankim Chandra Chatterjee

Lord Mahadev and his wife Devi Parvati lived on Mount Kailash, surrounded by lush green Deodars. Once the divine couple was playing a game of dice. The stake was a golden sphere.

Now the truth was, that however he played, Mahadev could never win the stake, while Parvati always did! Whatever the game might be, she was unrivalled at weeping, having superhuman capacity for it. If a high throw fell for Mahadev, she created a scene with her loud cries. And when a low number fell for herself, she would cast a glance at her husband, powerful enough to destroy the universe. So, even if he got the winning throw, Mahadev pretended not to notice it, and always lost the stake.

That day too, Mahadev lost the stake and Parvati got the golden sphere. And the moment she got it, she threw it down to earth.

"Why have you thrown away my gift?" Mahadev frowned.

Parvati won the golden sphere, but threw it down to earth.

"Lord, I am sure your sphere has some wonderful powers. I have not thrown it away. I have sent it to earth to benefit mankind," replied Parvati.

"No good can result from opposing the laws by which Brahma, Vishnu and I have created the universe. Prosperity and happiness come only by following these laws. A golden sphere can serve no purpose. If because of its beneficent property, the laws are broken, it will injure mankind. Come, sit here and watch how it works."

Mahadev and Parvati watched the drama unfolding on earth.

Thirty-five years old Kali Kanta Babu was a man of good position in the society. Some years earlier he had married the second time. He was on his way to visit his wife, eighteen-years old Kama Sundari, who was staying at her father's house. They were a wealthy family, living in a village on the banks of river Ganga.

Leaving the boat moored at the riverbank, Kali Kanta set out on foot to his father-in-law's house. He was accompanied by his man-servant Rama, carrying his suitcase.

Kali Kanta Babu noticed a golden sphere lying on the

path. Picking it up in astonishment, he handed it to Rama, saying, "This sphere seems to be made of gold. If someone enquires about it, I will give it to him. Otherwise, I will take it home. Keep it carefully."

Rama put down the suitcase and hid the sphere in his clothes. But then, he did not pick up the suitcase again. In fact, Kali Kanta Babu picked it up and carried it. Rama went on in front, the Babu followed.

As if this was not enough, Rama called out to Babu, "Hey you, Rama!"

Babu promptly responded, "What do you wish, Sir?"

"You are an ill-mannered fellow. Be careful of your manners in my father-in-law's house. They are gentle folk."

"Yes Sir. How can I dare to misbehave in your presence!"

Back in Kailash, Parvati was shocked to see this. "My Lord, I can't understand this at all! What is happening? Is it because of your golden sphere?"

Mahadev answered, "It is the special power of the golden sphere to exchange mental personalities. If I were to place this sphere in Nandi's hands, he would think he is Mahadev and would treat me as Nandi. And I would think myself as Nandi and believe Nandi to be Mahadev. Rama thinks he is Kali Kanta Babu and takes Babu to be the servant Rama. While Kali Kanta thinks he is Rama, the manservant, and takes Rama to be Kali Kanta Babu."

Back on earth, when Kali Kanta Babu reached his father-in-law's house, the confusion began.

Gatekeeper Ram Din saw Rama going up to the main porch of the house.He tried to stop him by showing him the place where servants were supposed to sit. Whereupon Rama replied angrily, "Mind your own business, you uncouth fellow!"

Ram Din then took the suitcase from Kali Kanta Babu, who turned to him saying, "Do not insult Babu like that! He will get angry and go away."

Now Ram Din knew the son-in-law well, but not the manservant. So, when he heard Kali Kanta Babu talk like that about the other man, he thought, "Since the son-in-law is addressing this person as 'Babu', he must be some one important." Thereafter, the gatekeeper addressed Rama humbly, with folded hands.

Taking full advantage of the situation, Rama sat down on one of the plush reclining chairs in the porch and ordered, "Get me a hookah!"

Udbhav, an old servant of the father-in-law's household, immediately brought a hookah, which Rama, reclining among the cushions, began to smoke.

Meanwhile, Kali Kanta proceeded on to the servant-quarters. Greatly amazed, Udbhav exclaimed, "Where are you going, Sir?"

Kali Kanta replied, "How can I smoke in his presence?" And this confused the poor servant even further.

Udbhav rushed to call his master. "Jamai Babu (son-in-law) has arrived, Sir, and another gentleman has come with him. Jamai Babu honours him so highly that he will not even smoke before him!"

Kali Kanta's father-in-law, Nil Ratan Babu, came out in haste. Kali Kanta, seeing him, prostrated himself at the distance and moved away. While Rama, coming forward, touched Nil Ratan Babu's feet, and they mutually embraced.

Nil Ratan wondered, "The companion seems to be a well-bred man, but why is my son-in-law behaving so strangely?" Anyway, he sat down to make polite conversation with his visitor.

Shortly, Bindi the maidservant came out to call Kali Kanta for lunch. He looked shocked and said, "Good gracious! How can I eat before Babu? Serve him first. Once he has eaten, I will come to the kitchen to have my meal, Thakuran Ma (mistress of the house)."

Bindi had never been addressed so respectfully. Feeling overwhelmed, she thought, 'Jamai Babu treats me as family! And why should he not? I also come from a respectable family, and it reflects in my looks, I'm sure. He sees all sorts of people and can distinguish, unlike the stupid people in this house, who don't know a gentlewoman when they see one.'

So, greatly pleased, Bindi went inside and reported that Jamai Babu's character was admirable. He felt that it would not be suitable for him to eat until his companion had eaten, and that the friend should be served first.

The actual mistress of the house, Nil Ratan Babu's wife, instructed the servants, "Let the stranger be served outside, and the son-in-law in the dining room."

Rama, seeing preparations for his lunch outside in the veranda, was not happy at all. "What kind of a strange treatment is this?" he wondered.

In the meantime, Kali Kanta was called in again for lunch. But he stood in the courtyard, saying, "Give me a little rice and curry, and I will eat here only."

Seeing this, his sister-in-law came out laughing. "What a lot of funny ways you seem to have learned!"

"Why are you making fun of me?" asked Kali Kanta, looking genuinely perplexed.

"Why would I make fun of you? Come, I'll take you to the one who has the right to do so." So saying, the sister-in-law pulled him by the arm and took him to the room where his wife, Kama Sundari, was waiting.

Kali Kanta, taking her to be the wife of his master, prostrated himself before her. At this, Kama Sundari laughed. "What new game is this?" she asked.

Troubled by these words, Kali Kanta said, "Oh! Why should you speak to me like this? I am your servant, you are my mistress."

"You are servant, I am master! Not only for today or tomorrow, but as long as I live that relation shall continue. Now come and eat your lunch."

"I don't know what people have told you about me. It's all lies. I humbly beg you to let me go."

Kama Sundari thought this was indeed a new sort of game. She said, "You are dearer than life to me. I can see that you have learned some fine jokes this time." And taking his hand, she pulled him towards the seat next to her.

The moment she caught his hand, he shouted out, "Help! Help! She is killing me!"

The frightened family came running at these cries. Kama Sundari, at the sight of her mother and sister, released her husband's hands. And he, seizing this opportunity, escaped.

"What is the matter, Kami? Why did Jamai Babu leave in this way? Did you strike him?"

Hurt at her mother's accusation, Kama Sundari answered, "Strike him! Why would I strike him?" And she started crying. "My sad destiny – some evil witch has destroyed me – has bewitched him."

Her loud cries attracted the rest of the people of the house. But they all said, "Yes, you must have struck him, why else would he call out so piteously?" The innocent Kama Sundari, thus reproached, shut herself in her room, to cry alone.

Meanwhile, as Kali Kanta came out, feeling all flustered, he saw a great commotion near the main porch. Nil Ratan Babu, Ram Din the gatekeeper, and Udbhav, were raining slaps upon Rama, who kept saying, "Let me go! I have never heard of a son-in-law being beaten so! Do you want to make your daughter a widow?"

Taranga, another maidservant, stood watching and laughing. Because it was she who had told Nil Ratan Babu that she recognised the guest as being Kali Kanta Babu's manservant Rama.

While Rama was being beaten, a distraught Kali Kanta, started crying, "How dreadful! they are beating Babu!"

At this, Nil Ratan Babu, became more enraged. He shouted at Rama, "You, scoundrel! What have you given my son-in-law to eat to drive him mad?" And he turned to his servants and ordered, "Beat the rascal with a shoe!"

At this command, a further rain of blows fell on the guiltless Rama. With all that beating, the golden sphere hidden in his garments slipped out and fell to the ground. Taranga quickly picked it up and gave it to her master, saying, "This good-for-nothing fellow is a thief! See Sir, he has stolen a golden sphere."

"Let me see it," said Nil Ratan Babu, taking it from her. Then, letting Rama go, he stood aside, opened the pleated fold of his upper garment, and cast it over his head like a veil, while Taranga, letting her *sari* fall from her head, tucked it up like a man's *dhoti*.

She was about to beat Rama with a slipper, when Udbhav said to her, "Hey you woman, why are you mixing yourself up with this?"

"Hey! Whom are you calling woman?" Taranga retorted angrily.

"You!" said Udbhav.

"Ah! So you mock me!" and, with the slipper in her hand, she struck Udbhav.

Poor Udbhav stood wondering at what just happened. Unwilling to strike a woman, he looked towards his master, saying, "See Sir, the shamelessness of this woman!"

But the master, pulling his veil a little more over his face, with a smile, said sweetly, "Yes, she is striking you, but do not be angry. She is the master and may do so, sometimes."

At Nil Ratan Babu's strange response, Udbhav became angry. "How is she my master? She is a servant, as am I. I am your servant, how can I be hers?"

As Rama was being beaten, the golden sphere hidden in his garments fell to the ground and was picked up by Taranga.

Again, smiling sweetly, the master said, in the same gentle voice, "What curious fancies we see in old men! My servant! How can you be that?"

Speechless with amazement, Udbhav wondered, "Have we entered a lunatic neighbourhood today?" And he let go of Rama.

At this moment, Govardhan Ghosh, Taranga's husband, keeper of the household cows, came up. He was astonished at Taranga's behaviour.

Taranga ignored him completely. While on the other hand, the master of the house, seeing Govardhan, drew the veil off his face and stood aside. Looking sideways at Govardhan, he whispered, "Don't get involved in that."

Govardhan did not listen to the master's words. He was busy watching his wife Taranga's strange behaviour and was becoming more and more enraged by the minute. Ultimately, he seized Taranga by the hair, "Vile woman!" he exclaimed, "have you no shame?"

Freeing herself from her husband in a flash, Taranga retorted, "Govardhan! Are you out of your senses? Go and feed the cows!"

At this Govardhan grabbed his wife and began to abuse her, whereupon Nil Ratan Babu exclaimed, "Heavens! That ill-fated wretch is murdering the master!"

Taranga, also becoming furious, shouted, "How dare you touch your master?" And began to strike Govardhan, left and right!

At the sound of such a fight, the neighbours, Ram Mukherjee, Gobind Chatterjee, and others came out to see what was going on. Ram Mukherjee, seeing a golden sphere lying on the ground, took it up and gave it to Gobind Chatterjee, asking, "See, Sir, what do you think this is?"

In Kailash, Parvati said, "O my Lord, take back your golden sphere! See! Gobind Chatterjee has gone into old Ram Mukherjee's house. Taking the old man's old wife to be his own wife, he is making sweet speeches to her. And her horrified maidservants are beating him with a broom. Meanwhile, old Ram Mukherjee, imagining himself to be the youthful Gobind Chatterjee, has gone to Gobind's house. He is singing songs to Gobind's wife. Soon he will be beaten up too!"

"Should that sphere remain a moment longer in the world, there will be confusion in every house. So, you must take it back!"

Mahadev answered, "Dear Parvati, what is the fault of my golden sphere? This is not a new condition of things on earth. Do you not constantly see the old setting the young in order, and the young doing the same to the old? The master behaving like the servant, and the servant in his master's seat? Do you never see a man behaving like a woman, or a woman like a man? All these things are constantly happening on earth, but no one seems to see how ludicrous it is. I have just made it evident for all to see. I will take back the golden sphere. At my wish everyone shall return to their own nature, and no one shall remember what occurred."

■■■

Fakir Mohan Senapati *(1843-1918), also known as* Utkala Byasa Kabi *or* Odisha's Vyasa, *was a writer, poet, philosopher, and social reformer. He wrote about common man and his problems and gave birth to the modern Odia literature. Senapati is credited with many firsts in Odia literary and cultural history. He wrote the first Odia novel, first Odia short story, first biography, and established one of the first printing presses in Odisha called Utkal Press at Balasore 1868. Senapati was one of the powerful writers who wrote against the cruelty of British rule. He also revolted against the conspiracy to suppress Odia language, which was going on at the time. It is believed that due to Senapati's establishment of Odia press, publishing of Odia books, newspaper, and literary magazines, Odia language was able to survive.*

Daak Munshi *is a story of the ill treatment of an old father by his English educated son.*

DAAK MUNSHI

(POSTMASTER)

An Odiya story

Fakir Mohan Senapati

Hari Singh worked at the General Post office of Cuttack. He had joined the postal department as an ordinary mail peon and thereafter, worked for a long time in various rural post offices. Finally, ten years ago, he had become a regular peon. At present his salary was nine rupees a month.

Hari's wife and son Gopal stayed in the village, while he himself lived in Cuttack in a rented room. Gopal was studying in the village primary school, with a monthly tuition fee of two *anna* (12 paise). Besides this, there was an added expenditure on slate, books and paper, every now and then.

Hari sent four rupees to his wife every month and managed himself within five rupees. It was his dream that with education, his son Gopal would become a successful person. So, he did not mind any personal difficulties, as long as his son's schooling continued. His definition of a successful career for his son was to see him as a postmaster somewhere, anywhere.

One day, the head postmaster, after examining Hari Singh's service records, told him, "Hari, you have already reached the retirement age. You cannot continue to work here anymore."

One evening, when the postmaster was relaxing, Hari asked him for help.

It was a shocking news for Hari. He had been thinking of bringing his son to Cuttack to give him English education. With the end of his job, that dream also ended. Hari started worrying about what to do next.

“The postmaster is a compassionate man. Surely, he would understand my problem,” Hari said to himself.

Hari used to visit the postmaster’s house every evening after finishing his duty at the post office. He would help around in the house, run errands, and fill up the *hookah* as well. One such evening, the postmaster was smoking the *hookah* and relaxing in a large armchair with his feet on a stool. Hari thought that it was the right moment to ask for help.

“Please sir, my son is still studying in school. I want him to finish his studies. But how will I pay his fees if I retire? Please allow me to continue working,” Hari pleaded with folded palms.

The postmaster had shut his eyes by now, but he was listening. “Submit your application and I will see what I can do,” he responded.

The postmaster had a good relationship with his seniors. Whenever they visited the post office, they would stay at his house. And as long as the senior officers stayed at the postmaster’s house, Hari Singh was given the task to look after them.

Hari knew the likes and dislikes of all the senior officers and attended to them accordingly. He even looked after them if any of them was unwell. He was so sincere in his service that he would go home only after the postmaster's guests were asleep, which would almost always be after midnight. Because of all this, the senior officers liked Hari Singh.

Following the postmaster's suggestion, Hari submitted an application for extension of his service. The postmaster added his recommendation to it and forwarded it to his senior officer. Finally, favourable orders were received from the headquarters and Hari Singh was allowed to continue his service.

Unfortunately, Hari's happiness was short-lived. He received news of his wife's illness. On rushing to his village, he discovered that she was dying of pneumonia. It was as though she was waiting to see him, before finally closing her eyes.

After the funeral, a devastated Hari returned to Cuttack with his son. Gopal started going to a middle school in the city. But then, how long could have Hari's service extension lasted? Ultimately, he had to retire.

On the small pension he received and by selling some of the household utensils, Hari managed to continue paying Gopal's school fees. While living a miserable life, he still believed that when his son would get a job, they would be relieved of poverty. So firm was his belief that he even spent whatever meagre savings he had on his son's clothes and books.

In time, Gopal passed the middle school. Hari promptly contacted the senior officers of the postal department, who knew him well. He requested them to give his educated son a job in the post office. The department bestowed its kindness and Gopal Singh was appointed as a sub-postmaster in the post office of Makrampur, on a monthly salary of twenty rupees. But first, he had to undergo a four-month training in a post office in Cuttack.

Now that his son had a job, Hari remembered his wife wistfully. Had she been around she would have been so happy and proud of their son's achievements! She was unlucky indeed, he thought and prayed for his son's long life.

At the end of the first month of his job, Gopal gave his entire salary of twenty rupees to his father. Hari had never seen this much money in his hand, his entire life! So, he kept counting it again and again in excitement.

He realised that his son was now an officer and was full of gratitude and happiness at Gopal's success.

An officer needs good clothes and shoes, so Hari rushed to the market and bought clothes and other accessories that he thought his son might need. Gopal Singh was Daak Munshi now, after all. And he wrote everything in English!

Gopal did well in his job and had officers as friends to socialise with. In contrast, Hari kept himself busy in cooking for his son, washing, cleaning and doing other household chores. He remained dressed as poorly as before and was only concerned with how to make his son live in comfort.

Days passed and Daak Munshi Gopal's attitude towards his father started changing. He would now get irritated by his presence, more so in front of his friends. Wearing uncivilised clothes, having no knowledge of English, the old unlettered man, loitering about in the house, his own father Hari became a cause of acute embarrassment to the son.

One day, it so happened that some fashionably dressed ladies were standing in front of the post office. And Hari Singh, clad in tattered clothes, passed by them. Gopal saw this from the corner of his eye and felt embarrassed. He decided to find a way to remove his father from his house to save his respect in the society he was moving in now.

That evening, Gopal told his father sternly, "You will not come out when my friends visit me. Who do you think you are? You have not done any favour to me by looking after me. If you want, you may live in my house, or else, just go away!"

Hari Singh was shocked to hear such words from his son. He went to his corner of the house and sat down on the floor, speechless. Tears threatened to flow from his eyes, but he quickly brushed them away, thinking, 'What am I doing? My shedding tears will bring misfortune to my son!' As that was what he had learnt from his ancestors.

The training period of four months had passed, and Gopal had to move to Makrampur. On the day of departure, he got ready early and ordered his father to follow him with the luggage.

Gopal walked away twirling his stick, while old Hari packed up their belongings and followed slowly. Weak as he was, and carrying heavy luggage, he was in no position to walk fast. After taking a couple of breaks on the way, Hari ultimately reached the Makrampur post office, incurring his son's wrath at the delay.

Things were no better in Makrampur. Gopal remained as ungrateful and abusive as he was in Cuttack. Days passed like this. Advancing age, hard work, and a broken heart, had taken its toll on Hari Singh. He fell sick.

Gopal threw his sick father, Hari, along with his cot and other belongings, outside the house.

One night, Hari's condition worsened. His persistent coughing disturbed Gopal's sleep so much that he called a peon in anger and ordered, "Take away this old man from here!" in English.

The peon was a simple uneducated man, who did not understand English. He only knew what was good or right and what was not. Going near Hari, he found that the old man was running a high fever and had not eaten for the past three days. The peon decided to look after Hari, instead of taking him away.

For a while, Hari seemed to be at peace, but then suddenly his coughing fit returned. This time Gopal lost his patience completely and threw his father along with his cot outside the house, himself.

Enough was enough! Hari Singh, with the kind peon's help, decided to go back to his village that night itself.

Once his health improved, he resorted to farming. He had two acres of ancestral land, which gave him enough to live comfortably. And he had his small pension too. He needed no one's help, least of all his son's.

Finally, Hari Singh lived in his village happily, thereafter.

■■■

***Rabindranath Tagore** (1861-1941), known as the Bard of Bengal was a poet, writer, song composer, playwright, essayist, and painter, who introduced new prose and verse forms into Bengali literature. Tagore was highly influential in introducing Indian culture to the West and vice versa. His novels, stories, songs, dance-dramas, and essays were about political and personal topics. He spoke ardently in favour of Indian independence, and as a protest against the Jallianwala Bagh massacre, renounced the knighthood he had received in 1915. He was awarded the 1913 Nobel Prize for Literature for his collection of poems* Gitanjali. *He was the first non-European to win the prize. India's National Anthem* Jana Gana Mana *is Tagore's composition as is Bangladesh's* Amar Shonar Bangla.

Kabuliwala *is a story about an unlikely friendship between a dry fruit peddler and a five-year-old girl, and the fathers' deep love for their children.*

KABULIWALA

(THE MAN FROM KABUL)

A Bengali story

Rabindranath Tagore

My five-year-old daughter Mini cannot waste a moment in silence. I really believe that ever since she could speak, she has continued to do so, not pausing even for a single minute!

My wife would often get tired of our daughter's constant chatter and would tell her to play instead. Sometimes, when her questions seemed endless, Mini would even get scolded by her. Then she would come to me for comfort.

I am a novelist and am mostly busy writing. But I always find time to answer Mini's incessant queries. I do not have the heart to tell my daughter to shut up. In fact, it is always the opposite. I love her curious nature and encourage her, resulting in some amazing conversations.

One morning, for instance, while I was engrossed in writing the seventeenth chapter of my new novel, Mini suddenly barged into the room.

Putting her little hand into mine, she started off, "Father, Ramdayal the gatekeeper is so stupid! He calls a *kak* (Bengali for crow) a *kaua* (Hindi equivalent)."

Without bothering to wait for my response about different languages, Mini continued, "Bhola says there is a huge elephant hidden in the clouds, blowing out water from his trunk! That is how it rains. What do you think, Father?"

Again, before I could come up with a suitable reply, there was another question, "Father, what is mother to you?"

I was tempted to say something absurd like, 'sister-in-law' but refrained and said, "Go out and play Mini, I have work to do," instead.

The window of my room overlooks the road. So, Mini just sat down at my feet near the desk, and started playing

Mini and the Kabuliwala often sat in the courtyard, talking and laughing, like best friends.

an imaginary game, humming softly. I continued working on my novel, where the hero was about to escape with the heroine from the third-floor window of the castle.

Suddenly, Mini stopped playing and turned towards the window exclaiming, "Kabuliwala! Kabuliwala!" Sure enough, in the street below was a Kabuliwala passing by. He was wearing the usual loose dress and turban that men from Afghanistan usually wore and carried a big bag on his back and boxes of grapes in his hand.

Just as I feared, the Kabuliwala heard her call and turned around to see where it was coming from. And I thought, 'He will now come in and my seventeenth chapter will never be finished!'

But the minute Mini saw the Kabuliwala's face, she fled in terror. She believed that inside the bag that he carried, there were perhaps two or three children like her! Meanwhile, the big man himself was standing there at the gate, smiling and saluting.

I knew that the only way I could get on with my writing was to buy something from the man and send him away. So, I bought some dry fruits. Soon we were chatting about the Russians, the English, and the Frontier Policy.

Eventually, when it was time for the Kabuliwala to leave, he asked, "Babu, where is that little girl?"

Thinking that Mini must get rid of her false fear, I called her out. She clung on to me, refusing to go any closer to the Kabuliwala. He offered her some nuts and raisins, but Mini was not tempted.

This was their first meeting.

After a few days, one morning when I was leaving the house, I was startled to see Mini and the Kabuliwala sitting in the courtyard, talking, and laughing. It seemed that in all the five years of her life, Mini had never found such a patient listener, other than me, of course!

The corner of Mini's little *sari* was stuffed with dry fruits and nuts. I handed an *eight-anna*(fifty paise) piece to the Kabuliwala, saying, "Why did you give her those?" He accepted the money. But, on my return, I discovered that he had quietly given it to Mini.

Rahmat, the Kabuliwala, began to come almost every day and managed to bribe Mini with his gifts of nuts and raisins. Mini had lost her fear of him and the two of them became the best of friends.

I would often hear them talk for hours. There were a few standard jokes that they exchanged regularly.

Mini would ask her new-found friend, "Kabuliwala, what do you have in your sack?"

Rahmat would add a nasal twang to his voice and reply, "An elephant."

And then he would ask, "So, when are you going to your *sasurbari* (father-in-law's house)?"

Unlike most Bengali girls of her age, Mini did not exactly know what marriage and going to one's *sasurbari* meant. Being somewhat modern in outlook, we had kept these things away from her. But she would not let the Kabuliwala see that she was confused with his question, and would counter with, "Are you going there?"

However, the term 'father-in-law's house' is also a slang for prison, a place where we are looked after well, without spending any money! So, shaking his fist at an invisible policeman, Rahmat would answer, "I will beat up my *sasur*(father-in-law)!"

Mini would go into peals of laughter imagining the predicament of the unknown creature named *sasur*.

I lead a sedentary life of a writer, but at the sight of any foreigner in the streets, my imagination transports me into their lands. The same would happen seeing the Kabuliwala too. I would be instantly transported to the cold arid lands of Kabul.

While I enjoyed my flights of fantasy and loved seeing Mini and the visitor from Kabul having animated chats, my wife was worried.

"Are children never kidnapped? Is it not true that there was slavery in Kabul? Is it absurd to think that this big man can kidnap our little Mini?" Mini's mother had plenty of doubts, which in any case, she had with most people.

I agreed that though it was not impossible, it was highly improbable. Anyway, Mini and Rahmat's friendship continued.

Soon it was January, and it was time for the Kabuliwala to go back home. This was the period when he would go from house to house to collect his debts. Though it was a busy time for him, he would still manage to meet Mini. If he could not come during the day, he would surely pay her a visit in the evening. Then the two friends, so far apart in age, would sit together to enjoy their little jokes. Their innocent bantering and laughter would fill my heart with delight.

One cold morning, I was busy working on the final pages of my novel, when I heard a commotion in the street. Looking out, I saw Rahmat being led away with his hands tied, by two policemen. The Kabuliwala's shirt had blood stains on them, and one of the policemen was carrying a knife.

I rushed out to find out more. The policemen said, "This Kabuliwala claims to have sold a Rampuri shawl to a man in this neighbourhood, who is denying it. There was an argument between the two, and in a mad rage this man stabbed him."

In the heat of excitement, Rahmat started calling his enemy all sorts of names. Suddenly, Mini came running out of the house with her usual "Kabuliwala, O Kabuliwala!" Rahmat's face lit up on seeing her.

He had no bag today, so she could not discuss the elephant with him. So, she jumped on to the next topic, "Are you going to your father-in-law's house?"

Rahmat laughed and said, "Yes, that is exactly where I am going!" But Mini was not amused with this answer. And seeing that, the Kabuliwala held up his bound hands and said, "I would have beaten that old father-in-law, but my hands are tied!"

Mini broke into laughter as the Kabuliwala was taken away by the policemen.

Rahmat was charged with murderous assault and sent to jail for several years.

Years passed and the Kabuliwala was forgotten. Leading a routine life in the security of our home, it did not occur to us how a free-spirited man from the mountains must be spending his life within the walls of a jail. I am embarrassed to say that Mini also forgot her old friend. New friends entered her life. As she grew older, she spent more and more time with girls, and even stopped visiting my room.

Soon it was time for Mini's marriage. She was to get married during the *puja* holidays. With Durga returning to Kailash, the light of our home was also to depart, to light up her husband's home. We got busy with the preparations.

Finally, the day of the wedding came. The rain-washed sun seemed exceptionally bright. The wedding pipes had been playing in the house since dawn. Each musical note made my heart throb faster. My Mini was to be married tonight.

There was a lot of hustle and bustle in the house. The canopy had to be put up in the courtyard, tinkling chandeliers had to be hung in all the rooms and the veranda. There was no end to excitement!

I was sitting in my room going through the accounts, when someone entered, saluting respectfully. It was Rahmat, the Kabuliwala. At first, I did not recognise him, because he no longer carried a bag and looked weaker than what I remembered. But he smiled, and all my memories flooded back.

"It has been a long time since I last saw you, Rahmat. When did you come?" I asked.

"I was released from jail last evening," he answered, smiling.

The words struck like a blow to me. I had never met a person who had been sent to jail for wounding another man. My heart flinched, and I wished that he hadn't come on such an auspicious day as my daughter's marriage.

"There are ceremonies going on in the house. We are very busy today. Can you come another day?" I said firmly.

Rahmat turned to leave, but as he reached the door he hesitated, and asked, "May I not see the little one Babu, for one moment?"

Poor man believed that Mini was still the same and would come running out calling, 'Kabuliwala, O Kabuliwala!' He had even brought some dry fruits wrapped up in paper for her, just like old times.

"There is a ceremony in the house, and you won't be able to see anyone today," I said again.

The Kabuliwala turned away sadly. The disappointment on his face made me feel sorry and I was about to call him back, but Rahmat was returning on his own.

"I brought these things for the little one, Babu. Will you give them to her?" he requested as he gave me a small packet of dry fruits.

I was about to pay him, but he caught my hand and said, "No, Babu, I do not want any money. You are very kind. You see, back in Kabul I too have a little girl like yours. It is remembering her face that I bring these gifts for your daughter, not to earn money for myself."

He brought out a small, crumpled piece of paper from the pocket of his baggy shirt. Unfolding it most carefully, he spread it out on my table. It bore the impression of a little palm. It was not a photograph nor a drawing. It was simply the impression of an ink-smeared hand laid flat on the paper. This touch of his own little daughter was what the Kabuliwala always had close to his heart, when he sold his wares in a land so far away from his home. The small palm print had kept the lonely heart inside his huge body soft and alive.

Tears came to my eyes. I forgot that he was a poor Kabuli fruit-seller and I belonged to an aristocratic Bengali family. No! What was I more than he? He was also a father.

I sent word inside to send Mini out to my room. Her mother objected, but I paid no heed.

Mini arrived. Dressed in the bridal attire of red silk, gold ornaments, and ceremonial make-up, she stood bashfully before me.

Seeing her all grown up and dressed as a bride, Rahmat was taken aback. At a loss for words, he could only say, "*Khokhi*(little one), I see that you are now going to your father-in-law's house!"

Mini now knew what the Kabuliwala meant and turned away blushing. The old joke did not work anymore. I remembered their first meeting and felt sad.

As Mini walked away, Rahmat sat down on the floor with a big sigh. Perhaps it dawned on him that his daughter

Seeing Mini grown up and dressed as a bride, the Kabuliwala said, "Little one, I see that you are now going to your father-in-law's house!"

too must have grown up in these eight long years, and that he would have to make friends with her all over again. And who knows what had happened to her in all this while!

The wedding music continued to play in the background, as the Kabuliwala sat lost in the arid hilly terrain of his homeland.

I gave him some money, saying, "Go back home to your daughter, Rahmat. Your joy at meeting your daughter will bring blessings upon my daughter."

Having spent out of my budget, I had to curtail on some wedding festivities. I could not have the electric lights or the military band as I had intended. But it was worth it!

To me, the wedding felt brighter with the thought that in a distant land, a long-lost father will meet his only daughter again.

■■■

Lakshminath Bezbaruah *(1864-1938) was a poet, novelist, and playwright of modern Assamese literature. He introduced short stories in 1889 and thus began the period of modern literature in Assam. Bezbaruah's short stories covered different aspects of the Assamese society, but with a touch of humour. He was honoured by the unique title of* Roshoraj, *meaning the King of Humour in Assamese literature by Assam Sahitya Sabha in 1931. Bezbaruah's writing always reflected the deeper emotions of the people of Assam. He wrote for children too, collecting and compiling folk tales of Assam and adding his own for the benefit of parents. Bezbaruah is also known in Assamese literary society as the* Sahityarathi, *which means Charioteer of Literature, for his expertise in all branches of literature, including writing patriotic, historical plays.*

Bhadaari *is a story of how a wife's generosity was successful in changing the mentality of her angry and cruel husband.*

BHADAARI

An Assamese story

Lakshminath Bezbaruah

It was like any other day. Shishuram returned home after a hard day's labour in his fields. He put away his plough in the courtyard and took a quick bath to wash away the sweat and grime. Wearing a fresh *dhoti* (loincloth), he went to the kitchen to eat. But he was in for a surprise.

Bhadaari, Shishuram's wife, was busy blowing into the wood *chulha*(oven), which instead of burning, was emitting smoke. The rice lay uncooked at her side, as did the curry and the *dhekiya* greens. The *kai* fish, smeared with ashes lay on the floor, uncut, while the curved *moida* (sickle) lay on a plantain leaf next to it. Clearly the lunch was far from ready!

Shishuram was already upset. The day before being the auspicious day of *Krishna Ekadasi*, ploughing was forbidden. This morning, the bullocks instead working harder to compensate for the previous day's loss, gave him a lot of trouble in the fields. To add to the irritation, Shishuram also had an argument with his neighbour Bahua, over an encroachment on his land. Things started going out of hand and the quarrel would have taken a nasty

Shishuram yelled at his wife, Bhadaari,
"Why have not prepared the meal? Can't you see it's late?"

turn had Bahua not fled the scene sensing Shishuram's rising anger.

There is an old saying that a man's rage is always borne by his wife. Once, on an earlier occasion too, Shishuram was angry with something Bahua had done. He came home and took it out on Bhadaari by beating her. His excuse at that time being, her not feeding the bullocks on time.

Bhadaari, like Mother Earth, always tolerated her husband's misbehaviour patiently, without any complaints. In fact, she believed that occasional beatings were as natural as hunger and sleep and were a part of normal married life. Her devotion to her husband remained unshaken.

But then, there is a limit to everything. Even Mother Earth trembles on excessive onslaught on her by humans. So, it was not unnatural for Bhadaari to speak up when things became intolerable for her.

With eyes and face flushed with anger, Shishuram yelled at his wife, "Daughter of so-and-so, why have not prepared the meal? Can't you see it's late?"

Bhadaari was already exhausted with her efforts at blowing the smoky fire. Turning to her husband with eyes that had turned red with smoke, she retorted, "Should I cook the food with my head? There's not a single dry log in the house. I'm blowing myself out trying to light the fire with wet logs. Is it right for you to get angry without using your head a bit?"

This was a highly unexpected response for Shishuram. His anger flared up further.

"What are you saying, you daughter of a bitch!" He roared as he rushed to his wife and struck on her back with the *moida* that lay on the plantain leaf. Before a second blow could be given, hearing Bhadaari's heart-wrenching cries, Kinaram, Shishuram's brother came in running. Seeing his sister-in-law lying in a pool of blood, he dragged his angry brother away.

Bhadaari was taken to the hospital. After three days, she came to her senses and looked around, hoping to see someone beside her bed.

She asked the attendant, "Where is he?"

"Who are you asking about?"

"My husband."

"Oh, that scoundrel? He is now in the lockup."

"Let him come here, Sir," Bhadaari pleaded.

"How can he come? He is in the police lockup. Don't think about him. If you do, you may get worse."

Poor Bhadaari became unconscious again. The doctor was called, and the attendant related their conversation to him. Understanding the issue, the doctor decided to get Shishuram to meet Bhadaari.

Next morning, when Bhadaari regained her senses, she was happy to see Shishuram caressing her head.

She smiled and asked, "How are you? Have you been eating regularly? I'm sure you're finding it hard to cook the meals. But don't worry, I will be fine in a day or two. I will help you then. Please arrange to take me home."

Hearing this, tears started streaming down from Shishuram's eyes.

Bhadaari called out to the doctor. "My husband is not to be blamed, Sir. He is innocent, spare him. It was I who stumbled and fell on the *moida* and hurt myself." Her eyes brimmed with tears as she entreated the doctor.

The doctor, the attendant, and Shishuram were shocked to hear Bhadaari's words. Shishuram broke down and wept like a child.

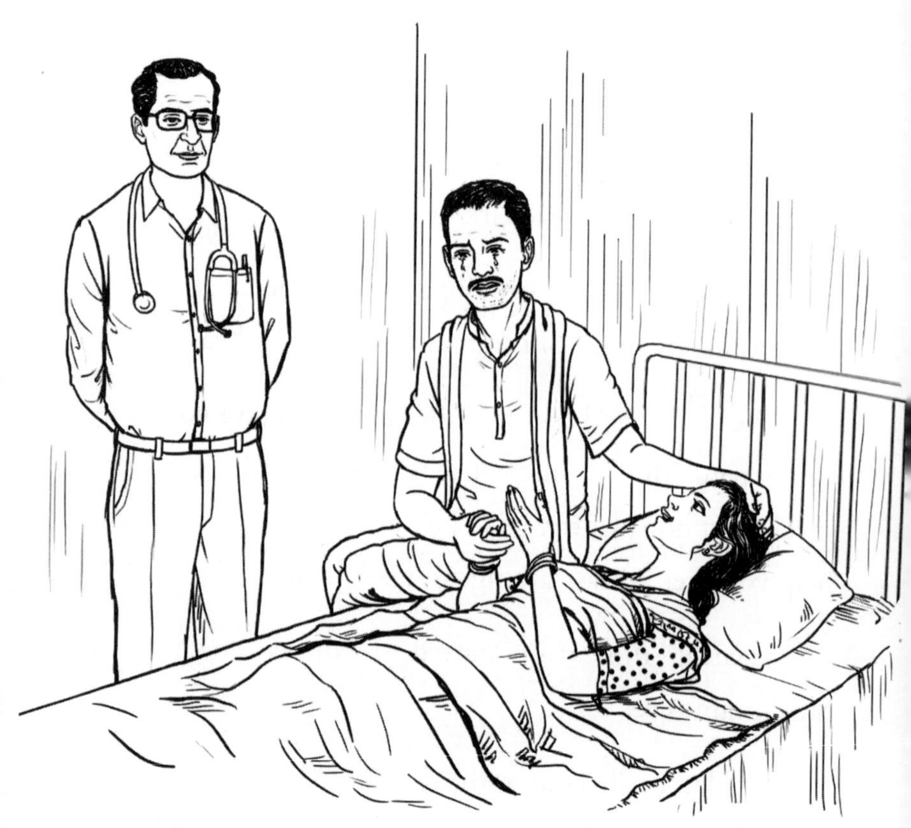

Bhadaari said to the doctor, "My husband is not to be blamed, Sir." Hearing this, tears started streaming down from Shishuram's eyes.

"It is not true, Sir! It is I who struck her with the *moida.* I am a sinner. I stabbed my poor devoted wife. I should be hanged!"

In a few weeks' time, Bhadaari's wounds healed, and she was sent home from the hospital. Though she tried her best to save her husband, the law took its own course and Shishuram was sentenced to three months of hard labour.

While Bhadaari cursed herself for her husband's plight, Shishuram happily went to jail to atone for his sin.

■■■

***Dakshinaranjan Mitra Majumder** (1877–1956) was a celebrated Bengali writer of fairy tales and children's literature. He wrote countless poems, stories, and biographies for the overall development of children and teenagers. Majumder travelled and listened to Bengali folktales and fairy tales being narrated by the village elders for ten years, recording them with a phonograph. Later he compiled and edited this vast treasure of Bengali folk literature, publishing it in four volumes:* Thakurmar Jhuli *(Grandmother's Bag of Tales),* Thakurdadar Jhuli *(Grandfather's Bag of Tales),* Thandidir Thale *(Maternal-Grandmother's Bag of Tales) and* Dadamashayer Thale *(Maternal-Grandfather's Bag of Tales). This was his greatest contribution to Bengali literature.*

The Lucky Brahmin *is a folk tale about how a brahmin is helped by his own good luck and his wife's presence of mind.*

THE LUCKY BRAHMIN

A Bengali story from Thakurmar Jhuli

Dakshinaranjan Mitra Majumder

Once in a small village, lived a brahmin and his wife. The brahmin was lazy and sat around doing nothing, while his wife took care of everything. She would gather fallen grains from the fields or beg for alms in the village. Sometimes, she would help other women in doing their household chores and they would give her food in return.

Though the wife spent her days getting food, cooking, cleaning, and washing, yet her husband remained ungrateful. Apart from not working or helping in the house, the brahmin was always ordering his wife about, demanding something or the other.

One day, the brahmin demanded to have rice cakes for his meal. This was the last straw. The poor wife was already tired and had blisters on her feet walking barefoot in the harsh sun. Her husband's callous attitude made her very angry.

"You good-for-nothing fellow! Get out from my house and my life! I am tired of doing your bidding all the time," she screamed at the brahmin.

Her scream was so loud that birds flew away from trees, and the trees themselves shook in fear.

The brahmin left the house and decided to become a hermit. It was not easy. He roamed the forests in search of fruits to eat. On one such day, as luck would have it, he met an old hermit. The man heard the brahmin's story about his wife refusing to keep him and took pity on him. He then took the brahmin to his hermitage.

The brahmin now began to live in the hermitage, listening to the sermons and gaining a lot of knowledge. In fact, he began to feel that he had become a learned man, and that everyone would be willing to keep and feed him. So, without telling the hermit, the brahmin quietly left the hermitage and returned to his village.

It was the peak of summer and even the pathways had cracked under intense heat. The brahmin had planned to go to the royal palace, expecting to be treated well, as was the custom of those times. The kings always treated the learned brahmins and scholars with utmost respect.

On the way, the brahmin decided to pay a quick visit to his wife and brag about his newly acquired knowledge.

The sun had just set when the brahmin reached the courtyard of his hut. He heard his wife cooking and waited outside. She had made a dozen cutlets, which she counted softly. The brahmin heard her. She was washing her hands when she heard the familiar voice of her husband.

The brahmin heard his wife cooking and waited outside. She had made cutlets, which she counted softly.

The brahmin was calling out to her from outside, pretending that he had just reached. Stunned to hear his voice, she rushed out of the hut.

"Where were you all this time?" she demanded to know.

"Oh, I went to study. I have become very educated now and have come to tell you so," the brahmin bragged.

The wife did not believe him at all. To prove to her that he was indeed a learned man now, he told her that she had made a dozen cutlets a short while back.

The wife was duly impressed and went running to tell the other villagers, how her husband had become a very knowledgeable man. The villagers were equally amazed as her when she narrated the incident of her cutlets.

Suddenly, the brahmin and his wife were being treated with great respect. People would often gift them produce from their fields, or sweets on festive occasions. Life became better for both the brahmin and his wife.

Meanwhile, word about the brahmin's superior intellect spread to kingdoms far and wide.

One day, a washerman in the neighbouring village lost his donkey. He came to the brahmin for help.

"I am a poor washerman. Without my donkey, how can I carry on my business? Only you can help me find it. Please help!" he begged with folded palms.

The brahmin told the washerman that he could attend to his problem only after completing his prayers. The poor washerman waited outside the hut, while the brahmin went in to seek his wife's advice. She told him to go out from the back door to look for the donkey.

Taking a stick with him, the brahmin left in search of the lost donkey, but could not find the animal anywhere. He returned and told the washerman that the gods were angry, hence the donkey had disappeared. Now the gods had to be appeased, which would take some time. The brahmin asked the washerman to come the following day.

The night was falling and the brahmin was worrying. He knew that if the donkey was not found, his reputation as a learned man would be shattered.

But then, he didn't know how lucky he was!

In the middle of the night, as the brahmin lay tossing and turning in bed, he heard a sound outside.

He woke up his wife, "Did you hear that? Do you think there might be burglars outside?"

"What do we have that they would rob? You are a learned man, think of a way to tackle the intruders!"

Chanting the Lord's name, the terrified brahmin stepped out of his hut. Lo and behold! The intruder was the washerman's lost donkey! The brahmin's wife quickly took the donkey to a corner of the courtyard and tethered it there. Telling her husband to go back inside and sleep, she went to attend to the neighbours who had gathered hearing the commotion.

The brahmin's wife told everyone that her husband had brought back the lost donkey with his prayers, hence the commotion, and that he was resting now. The people were astounded. The news spread like wildfire.

Early next morning, the washerman came rushing to the brahmin's house laden with baskets of fresh fruits and vegetables. His joy knew no bounds on seeing his lost donkey quietly tethered in the brahmin's courtyard.

The news of the brahmin finding a lost donkey through prayers also reached the king. It so happened that his daughter had lost a precious gold necklace. All efforts to find it had failed. So naturally, everyone advised him to seek the brahmin's help as the last resort.

The brahmin was called upon to find the lost necklace of the princess. As he was being escorted to the royal palace, the poor man felt that he was better off uneducated! To make matters worse, the king warned the brahmin that he would be imprisoned for life if he could not prove his knowledge by retrieving the lost necklace.

The scared brahmin begged the king to give him two days to find the necklace. "It is so precious that it would need more prayers, Your Majesty."

The king agreed and the brahmin was taken to the guest wing of the palace. The day rolled into night. The poor brahmin kept on pacing the floor of his room, cursing his luck.

But of course, he didn't know how things were going to change!

The nervous brahmin stepped out into the royal gardens and started walking, mumbling under his breath, "O Ma Jagdamba, why are you making me go through such trials?"

While the brahmin was talking so, the royal gardener's wife by the name of Jagdamba was passing by. Hearing her name, she got scared.

"Please do not tell the king anything, I beg you!"

The brahmin had no idea what she meant. She then confessed that she was the one who had stolen the princess' necklace.

The brahmin now realised that she must have heard his prayer to Goddess Jagdamba and mistakenly thought that he was talking to her. He quickly took advantage of that misunderstanding and assured her, “I will not tell anyone that you are the thief if you return the necklace. But do it the way I tell you.”

The brahmin dug out the pot from under a tree. The king's men broke open the pot and found the stolen necklace.

The brahmin then instructed her to put the necklace in an earthen pot, seal it, and leave it under the Peepal tree by the side of the lake. Jagdamba heaved a sigh of relief and did as she was told.

Next morning, the brahmin went to the king and told him that his prayers have been answered and that the lost necklace has been found. He then went on to describe the location where the necklace was hidden.

The king immediately sent his men to look for the necklace, but they returned empty-handed. This made the king very angry indeed. He ordered the brahmin to be imprisoned for life.

"Kind Sire, please let me go with your men to look for the necklace. I know that I will find it. Just give me one chance," the poor brahmin pleaded.

The king agreed to send him with his men. This time, the brahmin looked carefully under all the trees near the lake. Finally, he found the pot covered in mud. The king's men broke open the pot and found the beautiful necklace!

The princess was overjoyed. The king was so happy that he appointed the brahmin as the learned master of the royal court. He and his wife were given a big house in the palace compound to live in.

The lucky brahmin and his wife spent the rest of their lives in luxury.

■■■

***Premchand** (1880-1936) born as Dhanpat Rai Srivastava, was among the greatest writers of Urdu and Hindi languages. He was the first writer to write in depth about the lives of the deprived sections of the society, the themes being of immediate political and social relevance of those times. His works depicted the social evils of arranged marriages, the abuses of British bureaucracy and exploitation of farmers by moneylenders. The adherents of Hindi literature call him* Upanyas Samrat, *the King of Novel Writing. Premchand wrote over 300 stories, 14 novels, many plays, and essays.*

Kafan *is the story of a low-caste father and son who have no money to cremate the son's wife, reflecting their state of mind as well as the state of society in those times.*

KAFAN

(SHROUD)

A Hindi story

Premchand

It was a cold winter night. Ghisu and Madhav, father and son, sat beside a dead fire outside their hut. The entire village was submerged in darkness.

Inside the hut, Madhav's young wife Budhiya was going through the agony of childbirth. Occasionally, she would scream in pain, startling the duo.

"It seems she's not likely to make it. Go in and have another look," Ghisu said to his son.

"If she has to die, why doesn't she do so? What can I do by looking at her?" Madhav answered irritably.

"You are a heartless man! How can you talk like this about her after having lived with her for a whole year?"

"I can't see her suffering, thrashing about in pain."

Ghisu's was a family of *chamars*, the lowest among the untouchable castes. Their hereditary occupation was tanning leather. The father and son duo were quite

On a cold winter night, Ghisu and Madhav, father and son, sat beside a dying fire outside their hut.

notorious in their village, because Ghisu would work for a day and rest for three days. Madhav was worse. He would work for half an hour, then stop and smoke his pipe for an hour. So, the two of them very rarely found work.

A fistful of grains was more than enough for them. Only after a couple of days of starvation, would Ghisu climb up a tree to break off twigs for firewood, which Madhav would sell in the market. After this, the two of them would loiter around for as long as their money would last.

It was not that there was any dearth of work in the village. It was a village of farmers, and for any hardworking man, there was plenty of work available. But the lazy duo was called only when one was willing to be satisfied by getting one man's work done by two.

Had the father and son been mendicants, they would not have needed to practise restraint and discipline to acquire contentment and patience; it was already in their nature. Theirs was an unusual life. They had no material possessions except two clay pots in their hut, and rags to cover their bodies with. They were free from worldly cares, though were steeped in debt.

People abused them, even thrashed them, but the duo remained carefree as ever. Actually, they were so poor that nobody could expect to get their money back from them! In fact, people would continue lending them money every now and then.

The father and son would steal peas and potatoes from fields, or even sugarcane, for their food. Ghisu had led this happy-go-lucky lifestyle for sixty years and Madhav was following in his father's footsteps like a dutiful son.

Ghisu's wife had died a long time ago. Madhav had married last year.Since then, his wife Budhiya had managed to bring some order to their lives and food in their bellies. Though it is another matter that the father and son had become lazier and more insolent. If at all someone wanted to hire them, they would demand double the wages.

Today, the same Budhiya who looked after them, lay dying in the agony of childbirth. And these two men probably were waiting for her to do so, so they could get to sleep peacefully. They sat before the fire, roasting potatoes that they had earlier dug up from someone's field.

"Go check on her. Sounds like she is under some witch's spell. The village exorcist will charge a rupee to treat her," Ghisu said to his son while peeling a hot roasted potato.

"I'm scared of going in," answered Madhav. He was worried that if he went in, his father would eat up most of the potatoes!

"What are you afraid of? I will be right here."

"Why don't you go inside?"

"When my wife, your mother, died, I did not move from her bedside for three days. Also, don't you think Budhiya would be embarrassed if I saw her lying like that? I've never even seen her face from behind the veil, how can I see her in this state?" Ghisu was right in pointing out the issue.

"I was wondering, what will happen when the baby is born... we don't have ginger, jaggery or oil, which is required on such occasions." Madhav had other worries besides his ailing wife.

"All will be well once the baby comes. The people who refuse to give us even a single paisa now will happily give us rupees tomorrow. I had nine sons and we had nothing in the house, but God saw us through somehow or the other."

The fact was that people who worked harder than Ghisu were not much better off than him. Whereas people who exploited the poor farmers were very affluent. Seeing this, it was not surprising that Ghisu had such a mindset. One could easily see that Ghisu was more intelligent than the poor farmers. Instead of joining them in mindless labour, he would rather sit with the idle gossips of the village. But then, he didn't have the will to follow the rules and regulations of those people too. Hence, while the diehard gossips were the bigwigs of the village, Ghisu was always pointed out as a misfit.

Anyhow, Ghisu was happy in his rags because he didn't have to do back-breaking labour, and nobody could take undue advantage of him.

Hungry since a day before, the father and son were eating the roasted potatoes piping hot. They had no patience to let the potatoes cool, and in the process, burnt their tongues several times. While they were gulping the hot potatoes, Ghisu recalled the Thakur's wedding that he had attended twenty years back.

The satisfaction of having a hearty meal, a grand wedding feast, was something to remember all his life. Its memory was still vivid in Ghisu's mind.

"I can't ever forget that feast and the way I gorged myself that day. I've never had such an experience after that. The bride's family had served everybody with puris – and I mean everybody! And the puris were made in real ghee. Chutneys, spicy yoghurt, plain yoghurt, three different kinds of dry vegetables, curried vegetables, sweets… can't even begin to describe the flavours of that feast! There was no shortage of anything; you could ask for whatever you wanted and eat as much as you wanted. Everyone ate so much that they couldn't even have a sip of water! And those who were serving food kept on doing so, even when we told them that we were full. Finally, mouth fresheners were also served, but I had no place left in my stomach for a betel leaf or a cardamom. I could barely stand! So, I just rushed to lay down on my blanket. Such a large-hearted man that Thakur was."

Enjoying his father's delicious memories, Madhav remarked, "No one gives us such feasts anymore."

"That was a different time. Everyone thinks of cutting corners these days. Don't spend on marriages, don't spend on funerals… ask these people, where are they going to stash all the wealth that they have fleeced from the poor? There is no cutting down on fleecing and hoarding, but when it comes to spending a bit of that money, they start talking of cutting down expenses."

"You must have eaten about twenty puris…" Madhav was still lost in his father's memories.

"I had more than twenty."

"I would have eaten fifty at least!" Madhav declared.

"I wouldn't have eaten less than fifty. I was a strapping young man then. You're not even half my size!" Ghisu retorted.

After finishing off the potatoes, the duo drank water and curled up near the fire and slept. Meanwhile, in the hut, Budhiya continued to cry in pain.

Next morning, Madhav entered the hut and saw that his wife and the baby in her womb had died. He rushed out to tell his father. The father and son sat outside the hut and started crying loudly. Hearing them, the neighbours came, and as was the custom, tried to comfort the bereaved. But where was the time for all these formalities? The duo had more pressing worries – to arrange for a shroud and wood for Budhiya's cremation. There was no money in the house.

The father and son went crying to the village zamindar, who detested them and had also thrashed them once for stealing and not turning up for work despite promising to do so.

Anyway, the zamindar asked Ghisu what the matter was and why they had come crying to him.

"My lord, we are devastated. Madhav's wife passed away last night, though we both tried our best to save her. Our family is torn apart. Now there is no one left to give us even a morsel of food. I am your slave. Who else can I go to for giving her a decent funeral?"

The zamindar was a kind man. Though he was upset with Ghisu, he knew it was not the right time to show his anger. He gave two rupees to Ghisu. Seeing that, the other merchants also gave money to contribute in Budhiya's funeral. Within an hour Ghisu had collected five rupees. He got grain from someone and wood from another. A few people also offered to chop bamboo for the bier.

At noon, the father and son went to the market to buy a shroud.

While one is alive, one doesn't have enough clothes – barely rags – to cover oneself, but after death, one's dead body needs a full shroud to cover it. What an irony! The shroud gets burnt with the corpse. Nothing is left. The same five rupees could have been used to buy medicines to save Budhiya's life… if they had it earlier…

Such were the thoughts running through Ghisu and Madhav's heads.

They roamed about in the market, looking at various fabrics, but found nothing suitable. The sun was setting, and the duo found themselves drawn to a toddy-house. With unspoken mutual consent, they entered.

Ghisu bought a bottle of toddy, ordered some snacks, and fried fish, and sat down with his son in the veranda and began to drink. After gulping down a couple of glasses, the two became quite happily drunk.

Ghisu wondered out aloud, "What's point of placing a shroud over her? After all, it will get burnt along with the corpse. It is not likely to go with her to her next abode."

Madhav looked up at the sky, as though invoking the gods in heaven, and answered, "It is the way of the world. Why else do people give so much money to brahmins? Who ensure that they get it back in the next world?"

"The rich have money to burn, so let them. What do we have?"

"But what will you say to people when they ask about the shroud?"

Ghisu laughed and said, "We will say that the money slipped and fell from our waistbands. We looked for it but couldn't find it. The people might not believe in us, but the same people will again give us the money."

Madhav also laughed at his unexpected fortune and said, "She was a good woman. Even in her death, she ensured us a hearty meal."

The father and son had finished half the bottle by now. They ordered two kilos of puris, with liver curry, chutney, and pickles. Both enjoyed a hearty meal like the lord of jungle feasting on his prey, having no fear of accountability or any sort of scandal. They had triumphed over such emotions long back.

Ghisu philosophised, "If because of her, our souls are happy, won't it bring her God's blessings?"

Madhav agreed whole-heartedly, "O God, you are omniscient. Please take her to heaven. Both of us are blessing her from the bottom of our hearts. I had never tasted such food as I have eaten today in my entire life."

But after some time, a doubt rose in Madhav's mind. "Say father, won't we also be going there some day? Suppose she asked us why we didn't give her a shroud, what will we say?"

"What makes you think she won't get a shroud? Do you take me to be an idiot? Do you think I've learnt nothing in the past sixty years of my life? Of course, she'll get a shroud and a very nice one too."

Madhav found this hard to believe. "Who will give the shroud? You have finished all the money. She will ask me, not you. I was the one who married her!"

"I am telling you she will get the shroud!"

"Who will give it? Why don't you tell me that?"

"The same people who gave before. Though this time we won't get the money," Ghisu declared.

The night was wearing on. The stars were shining brightly in the sky. The atmosphere in the toddy-house was getting more and more intoxicating. Some people were speaking boisterously… some were singing and some

Ghisu bought a bottle of toddy, ordered some food, and sat down with his son to enjoy a hearty meal.

laughing. The worries of their lives brought these people to this place. Once there, they forgot their worries, they even forgot whether they were dead or alive.

Ghisu and Madhav were still busy eating and drinking, while others watched them in envy – how lucky to have one whole bottle between two men!

After the two had eaten their fill, Madhav gave the leftovers to a beggar, and for the first time in his life, experienced the joy and satisfaction of giving.

"Eat your fill and give your blessings. She, who is earning this, is dead, but your blessings will surely reach her. You must bless her sincerely, as this is hard-earned money."

Madhav looked up at the sky again. "She will certainly go to heaven and live like a queen there."

"Yes son, she will certainly go to heaven. She never bothered or hurt anyone. Even in her death, she managed to fulfil our dearest wish. If she won't go to heaven, who will? These fat people who fleece the poor and wash their sins by bathing in Ganga and offer its holy water in the temples?"

The mood suddenly changed, as is typical with intoxication. The happiness was replaced by sorrow.

"But father, the poor woman went through such hardships all her life and suffered till her death," Madhav started sobbing.

"Don't cry my son. You should be happy that she is free from this world of *maya*(illusion). She was fortunate to be able to escape from this illusory world so soon, to break free from the mortal ties of this life." Ghisu tried to console his son.

Both stood up and began singing, "Enchantress! Dazzle us not with your eyes..." and danced their hearts out, till they fell down in drunken stupor.

■■■

Gaurishankar Govardhanram Joshi 'Dhumketu' *(1892-1965) is considered as one of the pioneers of Gujarati short stories. He wrote over 500 short stories, 29 historical novels, 7 social novels, numerous plays, travelogues, essays, and memoirs. Throughout his schooling, his studying Sanskrit and literature in university, and his career as a schoolteacher, Dhumketu always had access to great literary works through libraries of educational institutions and wealthy patrons. Dhumketu's work was notable in the respect that he explored the inner worlds of his characters through their experiences of external events. His characters were frequently from the lower classes and castes, a section that had been largely neglected in Gujarati literature till then. He also deviated from the norm of the traditional gender roles by making his women characters strong and independent minded and men as emotionally sensitive.*

The Post Office *is a story of a lonely old man waiting, in vain, for his daughter's letter. It deals with a father's longing for a lost daughter's love and the world's indifference to and derision of such a deeply personal need.*

THE POST OFFICE

A Gujarati story

Gaurishankar Govardhanram Joshi
'Dhumketu'

It was early dawn. The sky was grey, and a few stars were still visible, glowing like the happy memories that light up a life nearing its close. Except for the occasional dog barking, or the twitter of an early rising bird, the entire town was wrapped up in silence. Most of its inhabitants were fast asleep on this intensely cold winter morning, barring a few women who worked on their grinding mills, singing softly. It was these sounds that helped old coachman Ali walk on his lonely journey.

Ali held his tattered clothes tightly to shield himself from the biting cold wind, as he walked through the sleepy town, supporting himself with an old walking stick. He plodded on till he came out of the town's gate on to a straight road. Now he slowed his pace somewhat.

One side of the road was lined with trees, and on the other side was the town's public garden. The sky had become darker, and cold, more intense.

Old coachman Ali's heart filled with joy on seeing the Post office.

At the end of the garden stood a building, beholding the wooden arch of which, old Ali was filled with immense joy, somewhat like what a pilgrim feels when he sees the goal of his journey. On the wooden arch hung an old board with newly painted words: POST OFFICE.

Ali went in quietly and sat in the veranda. The voices of people busy in their routine work could be heard faintly through the wall.

Name after name rang out from inside, as the clerk read out the addresses on the letters before giving them to the waiting postmen. With experience, he had acquired great speed in reading out the titles... police superintendent, commissioner, superintendent, diwan sahib, librarian... and then flinging the letters out to the relevant postmen.

Ali was listening carefully... but for the faith and love that warmed him, he could not have borne the bitter cold.

Suddenly, in the middle of the routine procedure of calling out names, a jesting voice from inside called, "Coachman Ali!" The old man got up instantly, and raising his eyes to heaven in gratitude, stepped forward towards the door.

"Gokul Bhai!" he called, opening the door tentatively.

"Yes, who is there?"

"You called out coachman Ali's name, didn't you? Here I am. I have come for my letter."

Postmaster Gokul looked around to see who had called the name. Sadly, someone had played a prank.

"It is the mad man Sir, who bothers us coming every day for letters that never come," said the clerk to the postmaster.

Old Ali went back slowly to the bench, on which he had been sitting for the last five years.

Ali had once been a great hunter. As his hunting skills continued to grow, so did his love for it. Eventually it reached a point that he could not live without hunting every day. His sharp eyes missed nothing.

If Ali sighted the earth-brown partridge, almost invisible to other eyes, the poor bird would be dead in the blink of an eye! Even when the dogs failed to see a hare hidden in the yellow brown bushes, Ali's eyes would catch sight of the poor animal's ears and the next moment it would be dead. Besides hunting, he would often go fishing with his friends. But when age started creeping in, Ali left his old ways.

Ali had a daughter, Miriam. She married a soldier and went off to Punjab. His daughter's leaving was a huge blow to old Ali, more so because he had not heard from her since then. It had been five years now.

Old Ali led a cheerless existence, waiting for some, any news of his daughter… waiting for a letter from her. He understood the meaning of love and separation now and could no longer enjoy the hunter's pleasure at the bewildered terror of the young partridges bereft of their parents.

Since the day Miriam left, a tremendous loneliness had entered Ali's life. Though a hunter's instinct was in his blood and bones, instead of hunting, he would now become lost in the admiration of green cornfields. He reflected upon life and concluded that the entire universe is built on love, and the grief of separation is inescapable. Reaching this profound understanding made him sit under a tree and cry bitterly. Since that day, he had risen every morning at 4 o'clock to walk to the post office.

Though he had never received a letter in his life, but with a devout serenity born out of hope and faith, Ali persevered and was always the first to reach the post office as it opened. One of the most uninteresting buildings in the town became his place of pilgrimage.

Ali always sat on a particular seat in a particular corner of the building. When people got to know of his habit, they laughed at him. The postmen made a game of him. Even though there was no letter for him, they would call out his name for the fun of seeing him jump up and come to the door. But nothing bothered Ali. With boundless faith and patience, he came every day and went away empty-handed.

While Ali waited, peons would come to collect letters for their masters, and could be heard gossiping. These smart young men in their spotless turbans and creaking shoes always seemed eager to talk about their masters. Meanwhile, the door would open and the postmaster, a man with a face as sad and inexpressive as a pumpkin, could be seen sitting inside.

One day, as usual, the clerk repeated his customary list of numerous names, police commissioner, superintendent, etc, and the peons for those people picked up the letters and left. At last, when everyone had gone, Ali got up too. He saluted the post office in reverence and went off quietly.

"That fellow," asked the postmaster, "is he mad?"

"Oh yes, Sir," answered the clerk, "no matter what the weather is, he has been coming every day for the last five years. But he doesn't get any letters."

"Who does he think will have time to write a letter every day?"

"He might be a bit touched, Sir. In his younger days, he committed many sins. Maybe he even shed some blood within sacred places and is paying for it now," another clerk added.

"Mad men are strange people," the postmaster said reflectively, resulting in an animated conversation.

"Once I saw a postman in Ahmedabad, who did absolutely nothing but make little piles of dust. And another had a habit of going to the riverbank to pour water on a certain stone daily!"

"That's nothing! I knew one madman who paced up and down all day long, another who never stopped reciting poetry loudly and passionately, and a third who would slap himself on the cheek and then cry because he was being beaten!"

Everyone in the post office began to talk about lunacy. As it happens in most offices, people have the habit of taking periodic breaks from work by joining in general discussions.

After listening for some time, the postmaster got up saying, "It seems as though the mad live in a world of their own making. To them, perhaps we too appear mad!" He left and the office became silent again.

For several days thereafter, Ali did not visit the post office. There was no one with enough sympathy or understanding to find the reason. Nevertheless, all were curious to know what could have stopped the old man.

At last, old Ali came again. It was a struggle for him to breathe. There were clear signs on his face of his approaching end. That day he could not control his impatience.

He went straight to the postmaster and asked, "Postmaster sahib, have you a letter from my Miriam?"

The postmaster was in a hurry. "What a pest you are, brother!" he exclaimed.

"My name is Ali," responded Ali absent-mindedly.

"I know, I know! But do you think we've got your Miriam's name registered?"

"Then please note it down, brother. It will be useful if a letter should come when I am not here." Poor Ali didn't know that Miriam's name was worthless to anyone except her own father.

The postmaster lost his temper. "Have you no sense?" he shouted. "Go away! Do you think we're going to eat up your letter when it comes?" So saying, he walked off, out from the office.

Ali came out slowly, turning after every few steps to gaze at the post office. His eyes were filled with tears of helplessness. His patience was exhausted, though his faith remained unshaken.

Ali heard one of the clerks coming up behind him and turned to him. "Brother," he said.

The clerk was surprised, but being a nice person, he stopped to listen to Ali.

"Here, look at this," Ali took out an old tin box from the pocket of his tattered clothes and emptied five gold coins into the surprised clerk's hands.

"Do not look so startled," Ali continued."They will be useful to you, and never be so for me. But will you do one thing?"

"What?" asked the clerk.

"What do you see up there?" Ali asked, pointing to the sky.

"Heaven."

"Allah is there, and in his presence, I am giving you this money. When Miriam's letter comes, you must forward it to me."

"But where... where am I supposed to send it?" asked the utterly bewildered clerk.

"To my grave."

"What?"

"Yes. It is true. Today is my last day, my very last, alas! And I have not seen Miriam, I have had no letter from her."

There were tears in Ali's eyes as the clerk left him and went slowly on his way with the five gold coins in his pocket.

Ali was never seen again, and no one bothered to inquire about him.

One day, however, life changed for the postmaster. His daughter lay ill in another town, and he anxiously awaited news of her. The post was brought in, and the letters piled on the table. Seeing an envelope of the colour and shape he expected, the postmaster eagerly grabbed it.

It was addressed to Coachman Ali.

The postmaster dropped the letter as though it had given him an electric shock. By now his haughty temper had been replaced by sorrow and anxiety, and his human heart lay bare. He knew at once that this was the letter the old coachman had been waiting for. It must be from his daughter Miriam.

"Lakshmi Das!" he called out to the clerk to whom Ali had given the gold coins.

"Yes Sir."

"This is for your old coachman Ali. Where is he now?"

"I will find out, Sir."

The postmaster did not receive his own letter that day. He worried all night, and getting up at three, went to sit in the office. 'When Ali comes at five, I'll give him the letter myself,' he said to himself.

The postmaster now understood Ali's heart and his very soul. After spending only one night in suspense, anxiously waiting for news of his daughter, his heart was brimming with sympathy for the poor old man who had spent his nights in the same suspense for the last five years.

At the stroke of five, there was a soft knock on the door. The postmaster was sure it was Ali. He rose up immediately from his chair, his suffering father's heart recognising another, and flung the door wide open.

"Come in, brother Ali," he cried, handing the letter to the meek old man, bent double with age, standing outside. Ali was leaning on a stick, and the tears were wet on his face as they had been when he last visited the post office. His once hard features had now been softened by the lines of kindness. He looked up, and his eyes had a light so unearthly that the postmaster shrank back in fear and astonishment.

Lakshmi Das had heard the postmaster's words as he came towards the office from his living quarters. "Who was that, Sir? Old Ali?" he asked.

But the postmaster took no notice of him. He was staring wide-eyed at the doorway from which Ali had disappeared. Where could he have gone? Finally, he turned to Lakshmi Das. "Yes, I was talking to Ali," he said.

"Old Ali is dead, Sir. But give me his letter."

"What! But when? Are you sure, Lakshmi Das?"

"Old Ali is dead, Sir. But give me his letter," said Lakshmi Das. The postmaster stared wide-eyed at the doorway from which Ali had just disappeared.

"Yes, that is so," broke in a postman who had just arrived, "Ali died three months ago."

The postmaster was shocked. Miriam's letter was still lying near the door. Ali's image was still before his eyes. He asked Lakshmi Das to narrate the last conversation he had with Ali, again. But he still could not doubt the reality of the knock on the door and the tears in Ali's eyes. He was confused. Had he really seen Ali? Had his imagination played tricks on him? Or had it been Lakshmi Das, perhaps?

The daily routine began. The clerk read out the addresses... police commissioner, superintendent, librarian... and flung the letters deftly. The postmaster watched them as eagerly as though each contained a warm beating heart. He no longer thought of them in terms of envelopes and postcards. He now saw the real human worth of a letter.

That evening, you could see Lakshmi Das and the postmaster walking with slow steps to Ali's grave. They laid the letter on it and turned back.

"Lakshmi Das, were you indeed the first one to come to the office this morning?"

"Yes Sir, I was the first."

"Then how… No. I don't understand…"

"What, Sir?"

"Never mind," the postmaster said, as he went back into his office alone. The newly awakened father's heart in him was reproaching him for having failed to understand Ali's anxiety. Now he himself had to spend another night of restless anxiety. Tortured by doubt and remorse, he sat down in the glow of the charcoal stove to wait.

■■■

Suryakant Tripathi 'Nirala' *(1897-1961) was truly unique. With a background in Bengali, he ended up becoming a renowned Hindi poet, essayist, storywriter, and novelist. Educated in Bengali medium, Nirala learnt Hindi only after his marriage. He is considered the father of progressivism, experimentalism, and new poetry, and is best known for his romantic poems. He wrote 12 anthologies of poems, 8 novels, 5 collections of short stories and many essays in Hindi. Nirala covered a variety of subjects in his works, like nationalism, mysticism, love for nature, rebellion against caste discrimination, sympathy for the exploited poor, and sarcasm for hypocrisy and exhibitionism. He gave a lot of prominence to* khariboli *or vernacular Hindi spoken in western Uttar Pradesh.*

Sakhi *is a story about a beautiful bond of friendship between two women, a bond greater than that between parents and children.*

SAKHI

(DEAR FRIEND)

A Hindi story

Suryakant Tripathi 'Nirala'

The young ladies of Model Houses planned to visit the theatre together. Nirmala, Madhavi, Kamala, Lalita, Shubha, and Shyama, all dressed up beautifully. As already decided earlier, they were to meet at Kamala's house.

Jyotirmayi alias Jyot had not yet arrived, and the time to leave for the theatre was nearing.

Lalita said, "Jyot looked very happy in college today. She was chatting and joking around with the girls, and then left early for home. And she most definitely wanted to go to the theatre! I had asked her why she was walking on air today, and instead of answering, she looked at me and laughed."

"Oh, she didn't attend the class then!" said Shubha, looking surprised.

"No," replied Lalita.

"She told me that her studies were destined only till now," Shyama added.

"But why? She is not facing any problems. Why is she stopping her studies then?" Nirmala was truly perplexed.

Shyama started smiling and answered, "She says, now she has to stop studying and start teaching, and has to make preparations for it."

All of them looked at each other and started smiling.

"What does it mean?" asked Madhavi innocently.

Shyama replied with a smile, "She is very concerned about teaching, because the student is an ICS."

"Really!" All of them exclaimed in unison. "So, this is the case!"

"Come, let's go to her house! Let's see how far she has progressed in her preparations," Lalitha suggested. Everyone agreed and headed towards Jyot's house.

All the ladies are students of Isabella Thoburn College. Some of them are in the second year, some in the fourth, some in the fifth, and some in the sixth year. Jyot is now in the third year.

After reaching her house, all the friends went straight to her room. Just like her name Jyot (means light in Hindi), her persona is also radiant. At that very moment, she was standing in front of the mirror and smiling. Seeing her friends suddenly like this, brought a blush to her cheeks.

"I was delayed a bit," said Jyot, giving no reason whatsoever.

She wanted to make an excuse, but her heart and mind were too busy to think of such mundane things. A strange and exciting feeling had filled her body, so much so, that even her softly spoken words could not hide it.

"Now all your works will be delayed, dear. Speed will only be seen while teaching the special student, that too without any payment!" Shyama quipped.

All the friends have a good laugh.

Lalita sees an opened envelope on the table and picks it up. Instantly, like a speeding arrow, Jyot springs towards her.

But Shyama intercepts her successfully. "How impatient! This must be the request to become your student."

Lalita started reading the letter loudly. Shyama held back Jyot. The letter was written in English and was longer than required. Byron, Shelley, and many other poets were referred to, even Vidyapati was not left behind! Jyot, who was held back, was brimming with happiness.

After having read the letter, everyone was ready to leave for the theatre. They decided to hire a *tonga* (horse-drawn carriage) from Aminabad. All of them couldn't have been accommodated in Jyot's car because the seat adjacent to the driver had to be left vacant as per the norm of those times.

Jyot suddenly remembered Leela. "Oh dear, Leela is left behind! Let us take her also."

"She was not asked earlier. It's doubtful if she will go," Madhavi commented.

"A typical miser, she holds her money tightly in between her teeth! She earns not less than a hundred rupees from tuitions but behaves as if she is penniless," said Shyama in her typical outspoken manner.

Jyot is embarrassed by this comment. "If you were to write her character-sketch, you would surely ruin it! There is no one like her in our college. Do you know who is the earning member in her family? She manages her expenses with the tuition money, pays for the education of her younger brothers, and manages the house as well. She doesn't want to trouble her old mother, and for that she works so hard. All that work is making her frail. Her eyes have become the prominent feature of her face now."

Lalita saw a letter on the table and picked it up. Jyot sprand towards her. Shyama held back Jyot, as Lalita read the letter loudly.

The ladies reach Leela's house. As expected, she was engrossed in reading.

Jyot grabs the book from her hand and keeps it on the table with a thud. "Miss Laila, stop being enamoured by tales of Majnu. All love stories end badly, my dear. Come, a Parsi company has arrived from Calcutta. Let's all go there and receive some religious knowledge."

Leela is pursuing her MA. She is two years senior to Jyot and doesn't mind her playful behaviour.

True to Jyot's description, Leela looked at her friends with large sad eyes and said, "You carry on, dear friends. Where do I have time for such things?"

"It's not time. Say it's about money," Shyama retorted bluntly.

"Alright, the issue is money. After college, I teach tuition for five hours. Doctor Sahib is a rich man. He is aware of my circumstances and pays me sixty rupees to teach his daughters. I teach Talukdar Raghunath Singh's new wife and get paid forty rupees. Our household expenses depend on this money. And after all this, I have to take out time for my studies as well. I am sure you all can understand my situation, and why I face shortage of time and money."

"Understood, Madam. Let's go now," Jyot insisted, "you will get a free pass."

"Jyot, you are glowing today, shining like the sword pulled out from its scabbard! What's the secret behind this happiness?" Leela asked her affectionately.

"She has become the wine that is gulped down and intoxicates the senses," Shubha said with a smile.

"Look at her – a smile dancing on her lips, eyebrows arched, a swag in her attitude – there is a Yes hidden in there as well as No," added Kamala.

"What is the matter?" Leela asked, looking at Jyot innocently.

"It's very secretive and poetic. All this debate is delaying us. The truth is that she has received a letter from Mr Shyamlal, ICS – a marriage proposal. And if she agrees, then his everything, including his three thousand per month salary, will be at her disposal. A permission has been sought to love and marry her. Do you understand now?" Nirmala explained Jyot's story correctly and briefly.

"Has your father agreed to this proposal?" Leela asked Jyot.

"If one is getting an ICS groom, then any father will readily agree for marriage!" Jyot answered with a laugh.

The room echoed with laughter.

"You all go. Please excuse me, I really don't have time." Leela was insistent.

"No, Madam. You'll get first-class grades while we'll be left behind struggling in mediocrity. Sorry, I will not let this happen! You must come. Go and change your clothes."

Jyot loves and respects Leela. Leela also understands that Jyot's free-flowing words reflect her pure heart that can readily share even her most precious things. So, she accepts her proposal, changes her clothes, and goes with them.

Normally, Leela's class gets over before 3pm. From there, she goes to Bhainsakund to give tuition to the Talukdar's wife. Every day she has to walk long distances. She can manage to buy a bicycle if she wants, but the thought of learning to ride it was embarrassing. So, she continues to go through the pain of walking.

She returns from Bhainsakund in the evening around 5-6 pm. Lately she has been observing two young men

Seeing the gentleman, wearing a hat and a coat, the ruffians turned back. Leela reached the man, frightened and breathless, and told him how the two ruffians had been following her since many days.

following her. Sometimes they walk very close to her, and her heart begins to race. But she would quickly walk away. As she would walk swiftly, they too would follow her swiftly. Whom could she complain to? Much of the path of Bhainsakund was deserted due to large bungalows and gardens. Walking with a racing heart, she would stop to catch her breath only when she would reach a village.

Deep within herself, she felt sorry for her helplessness. Everyone harassed the weak. But she had to keep quiet, as that was the only solution. She didn't tell her mother about it, for if she stopped her from going, then how would the expenses be managed?

One day, while she was returning, she heard one of the two young men mouthing obscenities, which seemed to be directed at her. She walked swiftly. They also walked swiftly behind her, till they were only 3-4 feet away from her. Then they dared to say such words that hearing them was beneath her dignity. She began to run in fear.

Luckily, she saw a gentleman, wearing a hat and a coat, coming towards her. Seeing him, the ruffians turned back. When Leela reached the man, panting for breath, she told him, "Since many days those two ruffians have been following me. I come to teach Talukdar Raghunath

Singh's wife. When I return from there, I find them waiting for me on the way. Today they said such words to me..." She tries to control her overwhelming emotions.

With the light falling on her face, the man could see her large tear-filled eyes. He angrily looked at the path and said, "Perhaps they ran away seeing me. My bungalow is close by. Please come, I will send you back in my car."

'But, then...' the man was thinking something as he walked ahead. Leela followed him. In the porch, near the garden, the man stood looking at Leela. The lamp post in front of the bungalow highlighted Leela's frail beauty, her beautiful fair face, with large eyes full of sadness. He asked her, "What is your name?"

"My name is Leela," she answered, lowering her eyes.

"And you have to look after yourself... are you married?"

"No. I am a student of Isabella Thoburn College."

"In which class?"

"I am pursuing MA," she answered shyly.

"Where do you live?"

"In the Model Houses."

The man looked a bit surprised. He asked, "Does a girl named Jyotirmayi also live there? She is a student of BA first year in your college."

Leela was also surprised. Gathering courage, she asked, "Sir, what is your name?"

"I am called Shyamlal." Then he turned to call his driver, "Listen, you! Bring the car."

Leela's hesitation had lessened, to a great extent. She said to the man, "I have heard of you."

The man grew curious. "Where?"

Leela smiled. "From Jyot's friends. They had stolen one of her letters."

"I have not yet received any answer from her. Her father had met my father when I was in England. Her photograph was sent to me. After returning from England, I wrote a letter to her, but have not seen her yet. Heard only praises about her." Shyamlal was lost in thoughts.

As she sits in the car, Leela assures him with a smile, that she would ask Jyot to write to him. Shyamlal stood silently with lowered eyes. Then he said, "No, please don't ask her."

On the third day, Babu Shyamlal received a letter from Jyot. It said:

Sir,

I did not write back because it was against decorum. Today, I learned about the chance meeting you had with Leela Didi. A Majnu always meets the Laila destined for him, like this only. Please look after your Laila, is my humble request to you. Then our relationship will become sweeter, because whom one's sister is married to, if he can call his wife's sister sister-in-law, so can the sister call him brother-in-law. I hope this relationship of ours will be long-lasting.

Yours,

Jyot

■■■

Amarlal Hingorani *(1907-1956) was a distinguished short storywriter in Sindhi language. Sindhi short stories began initially on religious themes with emphasis on moral values, but soon the focus moved to historical and social themes. Hingorani is known for his realistic portrayal of characters. His story Addo Abdul Rahman was recognised and included by UNESCO in one of its publications.*

Addo Abdul Rahman *is the story of a Sufi mystic who is given to converse with himself about events around him. Hingorani has effectively used this character to criticise a section of powerful people who enjoy social respectability because of their position.*

ADDO ABDUL RAHMAN

A Sindhi story

Amarlal Hingorani

The story of Addo Abdul Rahman is a true one.

Abdul Rahman was a tall and lean man of unknown origin and age. He lived in the city of Sukkur in Sindh, and roamed around aimlessly, on his own, wrapped up in a light quilt. Some people thought him to be out of his mind or mad. But since he could be seen visiting temples and shrines of all religions, many considered him to be a wandering fakir and addressed him as Addo Abdul Rahman. Addo means brother in Sindhi.

Those days, people often got together to discuss and recite religious poets like Sami. Rahman would join such gatherings to listen. Sometimes he would mumble to himself, "Addo Abdul Rahman, are you able to understand all this?"

Now Abdul Rahman had this unusual habit of talking to himself. It was not just mumbling, but actual serious conversations with himself like those between a person and his teacher or master. For example, if someone asked Rahman if he was hungry, his reaction would be something like this…

He would turn to himself and ask, “Addo Abdul Rahman, he wants to know if you are hungry and would like to eat.” And then, after thinking for a moment, he would answer, sometimes quoting a proverb, “One must eat to live, not live to eat.” It was as though he was consulting himself.

Rahman's life was full of interesting incidents. One day, he tripped over a stone while walking. There was nothing unusual about it. But Rahman said to himself, “Addo Abdul Rahman, how proud and arrogant you are! Walking with your head held so high! If you look down, you would not stumble.” He had barely walked a few steps, when he stopped and said, “Addo Abdul Rahman, how selfish you are! Was it right to leave that stone where it was? Someone else might trip over it.” Then after a pause, he added solemnly, “Addo Abdul Rahman, if you are a good person, you will pick up that stone and throw it aside.” So, Rahman went back and flung the stone out of the way.

Rahman tripped over a stone while walking and said to himself, "Addo Abdul Rahman, how proud and arrogant you are! Walking with your head held so high! If you look down, you would not stumble."

He may sound to be crazy, but Rahman was an accomplished scholar and poet, adept in Persian, Sanskrit and Urdu. He had studied Hafiz, Shah Abdul Latif, and Sami, as well as Saint Sachal. So helpful was he that when people received letters in Urdu, he would read and interpret for them.

Addo Rahman was a simple, quiet, and gentle person. He ate little and wanted nothing from anyone. His sole possession, the quilt, was his everything. Whatever the weather, hot or cold, one would always see Rahman wrapped up in that old quilt.

One day, an innocent man found himself involved in a criminal case of petty thieving. He was accused of stealing a rich merchant's gold watch. The police had searched him in front of people and found the watch in his pocket. The man seemed to be guilty without any doubt, but he insisted that he was being falsely accused and framed by the merchant himself.

The story was that the man was passing by the merchant's house. Somehow, the merchant felt that the man was making rude gestures to the women of his house.

Consequently, the poor man was beaten up mercilessly by the merchant. He would have died had Rahman not appeared on the scene by chance.

The merchant stuck to his stance that the man was evil and had dishonoured his family, and hence deserved to die.

Rahman, as usual, began to hold a conference with himself. "Addo Abdul Rahman, the merchant will not desist. His honour is very dear to him. He has a 35-year-old unmarried sister, for whom he will not find a husband because he will have to pay a dowry…" Rahman paused briefly here and then told himself, "No, Addo Abdul Rahman, do not lift the curtain from other people's affairs. It would be better to reason out with the merchant again. If he refuses, then you may speak the whole truth."

Hearing this, the merchant immediately decided to drop his case against the poor man. But unfortunately, others besides the merchant had also heard Rahman. So, the whole town began to gossip about the merchant, which was something that he did not like. He decided to file a complaint against the man again.

On being summoned by the court, Rahman told himself, "Addo Abdul Rahman, you have been summoned by the court of justice. Such a place is worthy of respect." It meant that he must not go there barefoot. Rahman managed to get a pair of shoes, and went to the court, wrapped up in his quilt, holding the shoes in his hands.

When he was called for evidence, Rahman put on the shoes, neatly folded the quilt lengthwise and put it around his neck like a shawl. He had barely stepped in, when a liveried peon of the court asked him to leave the shoes outside, as was normally done by poor people.

"Addo Abdul Rahman, the court peon is asking you to enter the court barefoot, to appear respectful. Tell him you got the shoes for the very purpose of being respectful." So saying, Rahman walked into the court with his shoes on.

The magistrate laughed on seeing Rahman and asked him why he was wearing a quilt around his neck.

"Addo Abdul Rahman, you are in the court now, so answer carefully. Tell the magistrate that it is a custom with the Hindus to wear a scarf or shawl around their neck

The magistrate laughed on seeing Rahman and asked him why he was wearing a quilt around his neck.

on important occasions. That is why you are wearing your quilt like a shawl." Rahman answered the magistrate in his usual manner.

The administrative officer of the court went to Rahman and administered the usual oath, "In the presence of God, I swear that I shall speak the truth, the whole truth, and nothing but the truth." Rahman repeated the oath respectfully.

Then the questioning began.

"What is your name?"

Rahman responded, "Addo Abdul Rahman, the administrative officer wants to know your name." Then turning to the court added, "My name is Abdul Rahman."

People at the court laughed. The magistrate was not very amused. A lawyer explained to him that Rahman was in the habit of speaking like that and meant no harm.

"Your religion?"

Rahman shut his eyes to think. The he said, "Addo Abdul Rahman, you have sworn to speak the truth. The question is awkward. It is better to answer in Saint Sachal's words: I am neither Hindu, nor Muslim, I am what I am."

The administrative officer did not know how to record such an answer.

"Write him down as a Muslim," the magistrate ordered.

"Your age?"

"Tell him Addo Abdul Rahman, that since the magistrate answered the previous question on your behalf, he may do the same with this one." Rahman was clear in his answer.

This angered the magistrate and he shouted, "You Jat! Make your statements sensibly and properly. Don't forget you are in the court of law!"

Rahman smiled and said, "Addo Abdul Rahman, the magistrate called you a Jat. Ask him what a Jat is."

The magistrate instantly reacted, "A Jat is an illiterate person, you fool!"

"Did you hear that, Addo Abdul Rahman? The magistrate says that a Jat is illiterate. By this definition, surely you can't be called a Jat, as you can read and write in five languages, Sindhi, Persian, Urdu, Sanskrit and Hindi. Will you ask the magistrate how many languages he knows?" So talking to himself, Rahman turned to the magistrate.

By now, the magistrate's anger had risen further. "A Jat is a person who does not know English," he declared arrogantly.

Rahman remained unfazed. His smile broadened. He said to himself in a confidential, yet loud enough to be heard, manner, "Addo Abdul Rahman, the magistrate says a Jat is one who doesn't know English. He knows English, so can't be called a Jat. What about his father Topanmal, the keeper of a cattle-pound? And his forefathers? Will you ask the magistrate, if his forefathers who knew no English were Jats, what does it make him?"

"None of your presumptions, you insolent rascal! Stop talking and submit a written deposition to explain why you should not be charged with contempt of court." The magistrate ordered.

Rahman wrote the following: "Honourable magistrate sir, Addo Abdul Rahman is not guilty of contempt of court. If anyone is guilty of such an offence, it is you. Your abusive language will not so much as touch the fringe of Addo Abdul Rahman's quilt. Let me give you a bit of advice. Though you sit in judgement over the people, you're not their lord and master. You are their servant. We witnesses have not attended the court of our own accord. We have been summoned to assist you in the administration of justice, and this is the way you treat us! Who will bother to appear in your court to give evidence if you abuse them like this? Will you show cause why you should not be dismissed from service for contempt of court? Addo Abdul Rahman has, in accordance with the oath administered to him by the court, spoken the truth, the whole truth, and nothing but the truth, so help him God. Signed: Addo Abdul Rahman."

■■■

Saadat Hasan Manto *(1912-1955) was a Muslim journalist, short-story writer and film script writer. In his early 20s, he translated Russian, French and English short stories into Urdu. Through studying the work of western writers, he learnt the art of short story writing. Manto wrote 270 short stories, more than 100 plays, many film scripts, radio dramas, and essays. His stories caused a stir in the literary world. Instead of imaginary characters, he exposed the ugly face of society by depicting real people, along with their psychological and emotional aspects. Manto is best remembered as the greatest chronicler of the partition.*

Shaljam *is a story from Manto's collection of short stories based on timeless comical day-to day quarrels between a husband and wife.*

SHALJAM

(TURNIPS)

An Urdu story

Sa'adat Hasan Manto

"Please have the servant bring my lunch. I'm starving," the husband declared as he entered the house.

"It's 3 o'clock. Where will you get food at this hour?" Pat came the wife's reply.

"So what, if it's 3 o'clock? I live here. I need to eat," said the poor hungry husband. "After all, I do have some rights in this house!"

The wife was quick to react, "Oh really! What rights? How many?"

"Since when have you started keeping track of such things – questioning me like this?" The husband sounded a bit surprised.

"If I didn't, this house wouldn't have lasted this long," retorted the wife.

The husband clearly did not want to argue. He only wanted food, and said, "Wow, you're amazing! Now, will I get my lunch or not?"

"You can forget about lunch if you keep turning up at 3 in the afternoon day after day. Even in a restaurant you wouldn't get *dal-roti* at this hour. I absolutely don't like your habits." The wife was relentless.

"What habits?"

"That you show up at 3! The food gets cold while I'm waiting for you. Only God knows where you are loafing around!"

Stunned at the accusation, the husband responded, "Well, don't people have work to do?" And then added patiently, "In any case, I was slightly late only on two days."

The wife refused to be placated. "You call it slightly late? Every husband must come home by 12 noon so that he's fed by 1 o'clock. And besides, he should be submissive to his wife."

"The food gets cold while I'm waiting for you!
Every husband must come home by noon,"
said the wife in anger.
"Shouldn't he perhaps live in a hotel?
At least the attendants would be at his beck and call,"
the husband retorted with a smile.

"Shouldn't he perhaps take a room in a hotel and live there? At least the attendants would be at his beck and call," the husband said with a smile.

"Wouldn't you love that! In fact, I'm sure that you're planning to take off any day. Well, you can leave now, right this minute!"

"Without having my meal?"

"Eat it at your hotel."

"But just now you said I wouldn't even get *dal-roti* in any restaurant at this hour? How quickly you forget!" The husband looked amused.

"You know why. Because I'm going nuts, or rather, being driven nuts." The wife was getting more and more infuriated.

"That's for sure. But who's driving you nuts?" The husband seemed to enjoy his wife's discomfiture. "You, Who else? You have made my life a living hell. I have no peace during the day nor at night!" said the wife, almost screaming.

"Never mind the day. But why don't you have peace at night? You sleep like a log, without a care in the world, or, as the saying goes, like one who sleeps after selling her horses."

"Who can sleep after selling their horses? What a stupid saying!"

"All right, it is stupid. But just a few days ago you sold not only the horse but also the horse-carriage along with it. And how nicely you slept snoring away all night long!" The husband continued trying to lighten up the conversation.

"There was no need to keep the horse-carriage after you had bought me a car. And the accusation that I was snoring is utter nonsense!" The wife retorted sharply.

"But my dear, how can you know whether you were snoring or not when you were fast asleep? Your snoring kept me awake the whole night, believe me," said the husband in mock earnestness.

"Wrong! Absolutely wrong! It's a vicious lie!"

"Okay, for your sake, let us just say it is a lie. Now give me my food!"

"Not today! Go to a hotel, as you mentioned just now… and you can live there for the rest of your life, for all I care!" The wife's mood had worsened.

"And you? What will you do?"

"Don't worry, I will not die without you."

"God forbid that you should die! But tell me, how will you support yourself without me?"

"I will sell my car."

"And how much will you get for it?"

"Six, maybe seven thousand, at least."

"How long will that feed you and the children?"

"I do not spend as much as you do. It will last me till the end of my days.And the children will not lack for anything either. You will see."

"Well then, teach me this secret. I am sure you've hit upon some *mantra* that doubles the amount. You pull out some notes from your purse, whisper the *mantra* over them, and they double!"

"You ridicule me. Shame on you!"

"Let's put this aside and give me my lunch." The poor man was starving by now.

"You won't get it."

"For heaven's sake, why? What have I done wrong?"Finally, the husband was getting exasperated.

"If I started to count your wrongs and misdeeds, I'd be counting till I'm dead."

"Look my dear wife, you have gone overboard now," the husband said sternly. "If you don't give me my meal, I will burn down this house! For God's sake, here I am dying of hunger, and you are rambling away this nonsense! I had some important work to take care of yesterday and today, that's why I was late. And you're accusing me of coming home late every day. Give me my food, or else…"

"Don't you threaten me! You won't get any food!" The wife responded stubbornly.

"This is my house. I'm free to come and go as I please. Who are you to impose these stupid conditions on me? I'm telling you, this attitude of yours won't get you anywhere!" The husband declared.

"As though your attitude has gotten me somewhere! This never-ending stress from you has reduced me to such a pitiable state." The wife had a ready answer to that.

"Some state!" the husband laughed. "You've gained twelve pounds while your crabby nature has ruined my health."

"What's wrong with your health?" The wife looked at him with sarcasm.

"Have you ever bothered to ask why I always look so tired? Or thought about why I am breathless climbing stairs? Have you ever offered to give me a little massage when my head is about to explode from pain? You are a strange life-partner. Had I known I would end up with a wife like you, I'd never have come anywhere near you!" This time the husband was ready with his list of complaints.

"And I would have swallowed poison had I known I'd be saddled with a husband like you." The wife was not to be left behind.

"Poison? You can swallow it now. Shall I go get some?"

"Yes, please."

"Okay. But first give me my lunch," the husband tried changing the topic.

"For the umpteenth time, you won't get it today."

"But surely, I will tomorrow, and every day after tomorrow because by then you'll be in the next world!" the husband couldn't resist joking. "Anyway, I can't go out for your poison on an empty stomach. Who knows, I might pass out and drop dead while driving! Looks as if I'll have to do something on my own to get some food," he added.

"Like what?"

"I'll call the cook."

"You will do no such thing!"

"Why?"

"Because I said so. You have no right to poke your nose into household matters."

"This is the limit! I can't even call the cook! Well then, the servant. Where is he?"

"In hell!"

"Which is where I am now too. But I don't see him anywhere. Move aside, let me look for him. Who knows, I might find him!" The husband still hadn't lost his sense of humour.

"What do you want to tell him?"

"Just that I'm letting him go and taking his place."

Meanwhile, as this inane argument was going on, the cook entered like a ray of sunshine.

"Salaam, Sahib. Begum Sahiba, the dish is ready. Shall I lay Sahib's food on the table?"

"Get out!"

"But Begum Sahiba, the *shaljam* (turnips) you cooked this morning are burnt because the flame was too high. Then you said Sahib would be coming late so I should prepare some other dish. Well, I have cooked two dishes. Both are still on the stove. If left longer, I fear they'll be charred like your *shaljam*. Just let me know when you want me to set the table." So saying, he left.

"Now I get it! That's what the fuss is all about."

"Begum Sahiba, the shaljam you cooked this morning are burnt because the flame was too high. So, I have cooked two dishes. Should I set the table?" asked the cook.

"What fuss? I get roasted in the kitchen all that time and it means nothing to you. You love *shaljam*, so I decided to cook some. Unfortunately, I dozed off reading the recipe-book and the accursed *shaljam* turned into charcoal. Where is my fault in all this?"

"No, of course not! No fault at all," mumbled the husband hiding a smile.

"All right then, get up now. Let's eat. The rats are gnawing at my stomach," the wife said as she walked towards the table.

"And there are alligators in mine," the husband added with a twinkle in his eyes.

"Will you ever quit joking?"

"Joking or no joking, come over here. Let me have a look at your *shaljam*. Let's hope they haven't turned into coals."

"We'll see about that after eating," said the wife, pulling a chair out to sit.

■■■

EXERCISES

Subarna Golak

1. "No good can result from opposing the laws by which Brahma, Vishnu and I have created the universe." Who is saying this and what does he mean by it?
2. Nil Ratan Babu and his family are termed as 'gentlefolk' by the author. What do you understand by it in terms of their way of living and behaviour?
3. What is the effect of Shiva's golden sphere on the people who are touching it?
4. Why did Parvati throw the golden sphere down to earth in the first place and why does she want Shiva to take it back from earth?
5. Shiva says, "This is not a new condition of things on earth." What does he mean by it? Do you agree with him? Why or why not? Explain with examples from your own observations.

Daak Munshi

1. What is Hari Singh's definition of a successful career for his son, and why?
2. Describe the strategy Hari Singh used to get an extension of service for himself. Was he successful?
3. How did Hari Singh manage to continue looking after his son's education and career?
4. How did Gopal treat his father after becoming Daak Munshi? Why do think he behaved in this manner?
5. What do you feel about the story's ending? Give an alternative ending to the story, explaining the reason behind it.

Kabuliwala

1. Why was Mini scared of the Kabuliwala, and what did her father do to get rid of her fear?
2. What in your opinion must be the reason behind the friendship of an old Kabuliwala with a five-year-old girl?
3. Describe the part or parts of the story that tell you about the writer's relationship with his daughter.
4. Why was the Kabuliwala shocked to see young Mini dressed up as a bride? What did he do thereafter?
5. Write ten lines imagining the Kabuliwala going back home to Kabul and meeting his daughter, and their interaction.

Bhadaari

1. Why was the lunch not ready for Shishuram when he returned home from the fields?
2. Why has the author compared Bhadaari to Mother Earth?
3. What was the reason behind, and the result of the argument between Bhadaari and Shishuram?
4. Why did Bhadaari try to protect her husband, and was she successful?
5. Was Shishuram repentant for what he had done? If so, what did he do about it?

The Lucky Brahmin

1. "Get out from my house and my life! I am tired of doing your bidding all the time." What made the brahmin's wife say this to her husband?

2. Why did the villagers treat the brahmin and his wife with great respect after he returned home?
3. How did the brahmin find the missing donkey? How did his wife help?
4. How did the brahmin find the princess' lost necklace? Who helped him this time?
5. What do you think the author is trying to say through this story?

Kafan

1. Who were Ghisu and Madhav, and why were they notorious in the village?
2. Why does the author call their lives unusual or happy-go-lucky?
3. Why didn't Madhav go in to check on his ailing wife?
4. What did the father-son duo do with the money meant for buying the shroud for Budhiya, and why?
5. What do you feel about the story's ending? Is it happy or sad? Give reasons for your answer.

The Post Office

1. Why did coachman Ali rise at 4 o'clock to walk up to the post office? Describe his journey.
2. Ali was a great hunter. When and why did he stop enjoying the pleasures of hunting?
3. 'He concluded that the entire universe is built on love, and the grief of separation is inescapable.' Who is the author talking about, and how did that person reach this conclusion?

4. Why did the people at the post office think that Ali was mad?
5. What made the postmaster finally understand Ali's anxiety?

Sakhi

1. The story starts with a group of young college girls planning to watch theatre together. Imagine and describe the same scenario happening in today's times.
2. Why do you think Jyot has still not responded to Shyamlal's letter?
3. Describe the parts of the story that tell you about Jyot and Leela's friendship.
4. Write a brief character sketch of Jyot, connecting her to the title of the story, 'Sakhi'.
5. The story ends in Jyot's letter to Shyamlal. Imagine the consequences and describe how the story is likely to move forward from there.

Addo Abdul Rahman

1. What unusual habit did Abdul Rahman have? Recount an incident from his life demonstrating it.
2. What was the story of the merchant and the thief? What role did Abdul Rahman play in it?
3. Why was Abdul Rahman summoned by the court?
4. Why did the magistrate get angry with Abdul Rahman?
5. Do you agree with Abdul Rahman's written deposition to the court? Why, or why not?

Shaljam

1. Why does the wife refuse to give lunch to her husband?
2. What is her grouse against her husband?
3. What are the husband's complaints against his wife?
4. What is the real reason behind the wife's unusual behaviour?
5. How do they finally resolve the issue?

ABOUT THE AUTHOR

Sunita Pant Bansal is a renowned mythologist, storyteller, and author with a career that spans over four decades. Throughout her journey, she has worn many hats, excelling as a writer, editor, publisher, and entrepreneur.

She has headed publishing houses and founded and edited newspapers and magazines for readers in India, the US and the UK. Her contributions to the world of literature extend across multiple platforms, working with prestigious organizations such as Walt Disney, Warner Bros., Pearson Education, The Times of India, Hindustan Times, and ABP Group.

In addition to her global collaborations, Sunita ran her own publishing house creating books for audiences worldwide and served as the President of the esteemed Institute of Indology, further cementing her influence in the literary world.

Bestselling author of *Everyday Gita*, Sunita has authored over 40 books for adults and young readers, delving into the philosophy of mythology. She has also written innumerable children's books focused on folk literature and scriptures, which have been translated into multiple languages and sold across the globe. Her books explore and reinterpret the timeless tales of characters from the epics and foundational texts for modern readers. Her storytelling blends mythology with history, making ancient tales accessible in today's context.

Sunita's contributions to publishing and literature have earned her recognition, including the 2024 AALEKH Women Achievers Award.

Amongst Sunita's recent bestsellers are Everyday Gita, Krishna The Management Guru, The Return of Vikram and Betaal, Puranas: The Origin of Gods and Goddesses, Ramayan: The Journey of Ram, Mahabharat: The Rise and fall of Heroes, Saint Kabir: His Life and Lessons, Tribal Revolutionary Birsa Munda, Boons & Curses in Hindu Mythology.

Website: *www.sunitapantbansal.com*

Social media:

LinkedIn & Instagram: *@sunitapantbansal*

Twitter & Facebook: *@sunitapb*